Midnight Candies

The Penstress

Conglomerate Ink

PO BOX 512 Shelbyville, TN 37162

www.rayneshapittman.com/conglomerate-ink

ISBN: 978-0-9967856-7-9

Facebook: www.facebook.com/ConglomerateInk

Twitter: @ConglomerateInk

Instagram: @Conglomerate_ink_

DEDICATION

This book is dedicated to my children and grandchildren. To my mother and father, my siblings and the man that completes me. To my grandparents who are now resting in peace. And I can't forget my uncles, my aunts, and my ex-husband. I appreciate and love you all.

MIDNIGHT CANDIES

Candy Apple

"Don't hang up that phone, Tony!" Jenna yelled through the bulletproof glass.

Tony didn't care what she had to say as he made sure to slam it as hard as he could on its cradle to show off his strength. He had only been in jail 30 days, but the weight gain looked good on him. The stress from being locked up and fighting a case normally would've eaten at Tony's weight, but he knew he'd fucked up this time and would be sitting his ass down for a while. He ate up everything they put in front of him to gain the weight he needed to protect himself once he made it to the penitentiary. Standing 6'2 the 165lbs made him look malnourished and the weed stains on his lips justified the claim. He was light in the ass but constantly talked that big boy shit that would land him in a lot of fights.

Jenna couldn't pin point how much weight he gained but she could tell he was healthier by the lack of jaundice around his dark brown eyes. She couldn't help herself as her panties moistened wondering if his dick gained weight too.

"I asked you not to hang the fucking phone up!" She said while laying her identical phone on the steel table in front of her. "I fucking hate you! Do you know that?!"

Tony knew it and didn't give a fuck because the feeling was mutual. Slamming the phone down was the only way he could show power with his freedom taken away. He was ready to end the visit but he wasn't ready to return to the 23 hours he spent a day in his cell. Putting up with her bullshit for an hour was better than the hours he spent daily watching his own back because of the charges he had over his. He'd kill his wife where she stood for the shit she did, but the glass only allowed him to stare at her hoping his look would commit the murder for him.

Jenna talked loudly into the glass never letting go of the phone she sat in front of her.

"How in the hell are you mad at me when you cheated first, bitch?"

"You started this shit, Tony. Don't hate the player; hate the mother-fucking rules of the game."

She hung up the phone, gave him the middle finger and left the jail house swearing never to come back to see his dog-ass. Jenna was fed up with Tony's bullshit. She thought she would never take him back after he cheated again, but the time had come to make a decision and she decided to stay with him long enough to settle the score before filing for divorce.

All she could think about as she left her dog at the pound was Ashley, the bitch Tony cheated with, and how it all happened...

It was summer in Los Angeles and everybody was out as Jenna drove down Slauson Avenue with her music blasting and her air conditioner on high. Even with shorts and a tank top on it was hotter than a hooker's ass on a Sunday, but it was summer, and there was no way she'd stay locked in her apartment while her man was out with his boys. She pulled into the Fox Hills Mall parking lot and parked in a spot she found just a few rows from the entrance and dialed her girl Toya's, number. Before it could ring, her best friend since their preschool days answered, "I'm right behind you."

Jenna had hung up, tossed her phone back in her purse, and checked her makeup in the mirror. Snatching the keys out of the ignition, Jenna made sure to set the alarm, so the carjackers wouldn't have it easy and headed toward the double doors.

"Damn bitch," Toya said out of breath. "You saw my ass damn near running to catch up to you. You could have waited for me!" The extra 20 pounds Toya gained showed every ounce of the 190lbs that she was made up. Lucky for

4

her the 5'11 frame she was built in gave room to spread the weight evenly. If it wasn't for her bull dog shaped jaws, her obesity would be considered thickness.

"I did, but it's hot as hell out there, and my makeup keeps sweating." Jenna laughed while wiping the sweat from her nose with a tissue. The makeup wasn't necessary but it did give her almond toned skin, a unique bronze tint to it. Her puppy dog eyes, pouty lips and oval shaped face were the real source of her beauty.

"Stop wearing that cheap shit you get from the 99 cents store and you won't have to worry about it sweating off. So are we eating or shopping first because my stomach's been growling all day?" Toya asked looking in the direction of the food court.

"We can eat first, fat ass. I ate this morning but I do want some pizza."

Toya came to a sudden stop, grabbed Jenna by the arm, and pulled her toward a crowd of people. "What?" Jenna snapped looking confused.

"Look."

"Look at what?" Jenna replied looking in both directions.

"Look to your left next to the man in the brown shirt with the Mohawk."

Jenna spotted the man her best friend had referenced and shouted,

"Oh hell no! I know that's not Tony's trifling ass in here with a bitch."

Toya looked at her side eyed and whispered,

"Yes, but if I wanted you to get all loud, I wouldn't have tried to hide you in the first damn place."

Reading Jenna's face, she knew she was about to hit the fan. "Stay here sis, I got this shit," she said making her way towards Tony and leaving a pissed off Jenna fuming behind.

"Hey big bro! Where's Jenna?" she asked sneaking up

and hugging Tony from behind while giving the woman with him the *bitch I wish you would say something* stare.

"Who?" Tony replied trying to play dumb.

"*Jenna,*" Toya repeated with a smile noticing the look of shock on his face when she said her best friend's name. Ashley, feeling the tension extended her hand to Toya.

"Hi, I'm Ashley," she said smiling.

"Hey," Toya greeted dryly before focusing her attention back on Tony. "Look, I don't know why you're up in here fronting like you don't know my girl or whatever, but tell her to call me when you get back home."

Jenna had seen enough and couldn't hold her anger back any longer. Her face was pink when it should have been yellow from being pissed off. She forced a smile on it and walked from the crowd of people towards Tony.

Ashley spotted her before anyone and noticed that she was the same woman from the picture she'd seen in Tony's apartment. Men lie all the time, so she made it her business

7

to snoop through his bedroom drawers while he was in the shower. After noticing a pair of panties behind a chair in his bedroom on her first visit she felt snooping was mandatory. She had a feeling that he lived with someone by the way his apartment was decorated, but Tony put her mind at ease with the lie that his god sister helped him and stopped by whenever she wanted. He fed Ashley some bullshit about them being best friends and that he and his sister were so close that people assumed they were husband and wife instead of siblings. Ashley listened, but his words didn't stop her from opening the top drawer to his nightstand. She didn't find anything in there; however there was but broken watches and men's cologne so she opened the bottom drawer and picked up a picture frame that she noticed lying face down on socks and drawls. It was a picture of Tony holding a woman from behind by the waist. They looked happy, not in love but hey, it could have been his sister, she thought. The shower in the next room was no longer running so Ashley quickly returned the photo to the drawer. Not wanting to fuck up a good day, she decided not to say anything to Tony.

Ashley wasn't trying to stare at the chick walking her way, but somebody needed to keep an eye on her seeing that Tony was still going back and forth with Toya trying to maintain his lie. The look on the chick's face said shit was about to hit the fan, and not wanting to be in the middle of any drama, Ashley managed to slip away unnoticed.

"What's up bitch," Jenna yelled slapping Tony across the face. "Nigga, have you lost your fucking mind? After everything I've done for your broke ass, and this is how you do me? You sorry son of a bitch walking around the mall with some rat-faced bitch like you got platinum dick. Nigga, please. You're a broke, can't fuck, can't eat pussy, and can't keep a job ass, nigga," Jenna expected for the bitch to speak up in defense but after looking around, her husband's side piece had disappeared. "You better go find that ho cus' she can have you and your fucked up ass credit."

"Man….what the fuck is wrong with you? You lucky we in public, or I'd beat your ass, bitch," Tony said as he rubbed the sting her slap left on his face.

"Bitch? Now, I'm a bitch because I caught your ass cheating on me again? Nigga, fuck you!" Jenna yelled in his face while throwing up both her middle fingers as he walked away.

"Don't trip off that little boy, Jen. He ain't about shit and you know he's not. Hell, look at all the times his bitch ass has cheated on you. Don't take him back this time and give him back that $30.00 ring. You think I can't see that shit turning your finger green!"

"I know you love me T, but I don't want to hear this shit right now. That's my husband!"

"You need to hear it because you're in public making a fool of yourself. You're calling that lame ass, nigga your husband but screaming he's broke and can't fuck in the same breath. Which is it, Sis?"

Jenna wanted to slap Toya but she knew she was right. "I don't know but I need to calm down. I'll call you when I get home."

"Yeah you need to do that too but give me a hug. You got the mall security looking at you and you know them flash light cops love them cops, play victim." Toya embraced her and then whispered. "If they ask me, I'm gon' say that nigga hit you first."

"Bitch, you silly."

"No bitch, I'm real. You better pull that hospital scene from *A Thin Line between Love and Hate* on his ass and you know you don't have to go home. You can come chill at my place until you figure this shit out. I got a bottle in the refrigerator and some loud next to the bed. We can get fucked up and go bust all his tires and windows out his car." Toya laughed but she meant everything she had said.

"Thanks boo, but I'm going to go home. I'll call you later," she said freeing herself from the forced show of affection and walked away with everyone in the food court eyes on her.

When Jenna got home, Tony was sitting on the couch watching TV like nothing happened.

"What the fuck are you doing here? You need to leave. Yo' ass got to go," she demanded from the doorway, with her hands on her hips.

"That wasn't my bitch Jen, you my bitch and why in the fuck do I got to go? I live here too!"

"I could have sworn that was your bitch. The two of you walking through the mall, arm in arm, giggling and holding bags. Hmmm, sounds just like our first date...except you paid for everything, which I know isn't the case because your ass is broke!" Jenna laughed.

"I don't see what you find to be so funny. You let that

ho Toya gas you up. She's just a friend from work."

Jenna laughed, "A friend from work? You don't have a job, Tony. Your mama told me they fired you two weeks ago, and you've been hiding out at her house scared to tell me that you loss another job." She walked into the apartment and started tossing everything in her reach that belonged to him towards the door. "What you need to do is get your shit together and then come back and play married with me. I'm not even mad at you this time. Just don't be mad at me when I'm in the mall, hand in hand, tricking' off on some other niggas money too."

"Man, fuck this! I'm going to my mama's house and if I catch you with another nigga, I'm beating his ass and yours. When you realize you're wrongly accusing a real nigga, shoot me an apology text and I'll come back."

"Boy, please," Jenna said rolling her eyes. "You ain't no real nigga. You can't even spell it. Go ahead and run to yo' mama's house. When I find me a real one, you and that bitch can join us. So tell your boo to step her game up because we not eating at the damn food court!" Jenna announced, walking into their bedroom and locking the door behind her.

As she picked up the phone to call Toya, she heard cabinet doors slamming and what had to be dishes breaking. She laughed until she cried. The nigga was having a temper tantrum like he was innocent, but his actions were an admission of guilt. Jenna had given Tony the best years of her life, and this is what she got in return. Finally hearing the door slam, she waited a couple of minutes then went to make sure the doors were locked. The bag that Tony kept packed by the door from being kicked out at least once a month was gone.

"Good, his lying ass can stay gone."

The following day, jealousy and insecurities paid Jenna a visit and left her wondering why wasn't she ever good enough for the man who begged for her hand in marriage? More important, what did the bitch at the mall have that she didn't? She needed answers, and Tony's phone records online would provide them. She wrote down every number she didn't recognize. Using her natural detective instinct to create a time she was sure the very first number was his food court bitch and if she didn't have her instinct, his 20 outgoing calls to one number from the time he left her at the mall confirmed it. She poured a glass of wine and sent a text.

Hey, baby. This is Tony. You're not answering my calls so I'm using my homeboy's line. I've been trying to apologize for what happened. Can you please stop by the house later?

What for Tony?

I need to explain things, baby that's why. Shit, you snuck off without even saying anything.

Your wife pulled up so miss me with the bullshit

Tony. You're fucking married.

Please just let me explain, baby.

I'll think about it.

Can we hook up later on?

I said, I'll think about it!

You know you coming cus' you miss daddy's dick.

Actually, fucking with you makes me wish I was chin deep in some pussy. You know how I rock, pussy first and dick third, lol.

Jenna's mouth dropped and she didn't know what to text back, but there wasn't a need to because the next text said it all.

I guess I can come ride that dick one more time. I love hearing you moan my name. You make Ashley sound like Ashy, lol

Jenna couldn't dial Toya's number fast enough.

"Girl, guess what?"

"What?" Toya whispered into the phone not wanting

the hoes in the nail shop to hear her.

"I sent that bitch a text, and pretended I was Tony. She's coming over later."

Toya gasped, "You did what? How did you pull that off and how do you know she's not going to reach out to him before that? Jenna, you are crazy as hell."

"She's not, I temporarily suspended his line and got her texting my number," Jenna replied, "and crazy don't even describe how I'm feeling. I plan on getting all the information Ms. Ashy is willing to give me so I know how much pussy I need to slang to the next," Jenna laughed.

"Did you say Ashy or Ashley?"

"The ho likes being called both apparently."

"Well make sure you let me know what happens."

"I will. I am about to see if I can find her on one of these social networks. She seems like an internet ho."

"Okay, Jen, I'll talk to your crazy ass later, and tell Ms. Ashy I said heeeey girl!" Toya said.

"Alright, bye." Jenna hung up and got online to find Ashley. She hadn't logged into her Facebook account in months because she found herself obsessing over every woman who liked one of her husband's post. She was convinced that every woman who liked his pictures wanted his dick or already had it and after beefing with his entire female friend's list, he blocked her. Good thing he didn't know she was cat-fishing his ass from three different pages one of which she created from a picture she'd stolen off his family reunion website. Tony wasn't close enough to his family to question the authenticity of his third cousin's friend request. Once he saw they had a few mutual friends which were all of his bloodline, he accepted it without question. That's the account Jenna logged into and went straight to Tony's page to roam through his friends. The only name that was even close to Ashley was listed as, AshIam. The profile picture was a tigress with her cubs. It didn't take long to run across a photo of Ashley to confirm her mark. The next picture to follow was of Ashley sitting on a masculine woman's lap in a bra and cutoff shorts.

What the hell? Is she tongue kissing a woman? Jenna thought looking at the picture that followed but that wasn't the problem. Two women kissing weren't surprising in this day and age, but her panties moistening from staring at Ashley's breast was. Jenna had never had a gay thought in her life, but for some odd reason she wanted to see if Ashley's nipples were as perfect the rest of the mounds that made her breast.

The time had come for Jenna's special guest to arrive. She ran herself a nice bubble bath, lit candles around the apartment, turned on some music, and left the door unlocked for Ashley. She didn't get into the tub until she received Ashley's text saying she was on her way. Ten minutes later, Jenna heard the door open and close.

"Who is that?" she yelled from the bathroom.

"Ashley... I'm... umm... Tony asked me to come over,

to drop something off," She stuttered as she lied.

"Can you come in the bathroom and hand me my towel, please?"

Ashley wasn't sure what to do next. She thought about putting her purse and keys on the table as she did what was asked but running out the front door before whoever the woman was in the tub crossed her mind too. She walked into the bathroom with her curiosity leading the way.

"I'm sorry; I'm not dressed. I hadn't planned on being in the bath this long and I thought Tony would be back by now."

"Damn," Ashley replied, standing at the door.

"What's wrong?" Jenna asked.

"Nothing," Ashley replied, standing in the doorway and staring at Jenna's naked body as she stepped out the tub. It was the chick from the food court, she was sure of it.

"Thanks, I hope you don't mind me changing in front of you. You're a woman; I'm sure you've seen tits and ass before."

Ashley laughed not knowing if she recognized her as well, "I don't mind; it's cool. So, where's Tony I want to give him his umm… money so he can leave me alone?" She wasn't a lie nor was she a saint but felt the need to confess anyways, "He never told me about you, I swear. That's why I bounced at the food court!"

"Ummhmm, you swear? I bet you do just like you came over here to give him his umm… money, so he could leave you alone, huh? Well, Tony is with his mom's where his ass can stay for all I care."

"Oh, okay. Well tell him I tried to bring it to him. I'll see you around I guess." Ashley replied.

"He didn't tell you where he was?" Jenna asked.

"No, I haven't been answering his calls and the only reason I came here was because he texted from one of his friends phone."

"Typical Tony…would you mind drying off my

back?"

"No, I don't mind but don't you think I should be going now?"

"Why the rush?"

What the hell is going on? Ashley thought taking the towel from Jenna.

"I mean, you saw us at the mall and snapped off. I don't completely understand why you're so calm. I mean, he is your husband and although I didn't know about you. I'm sure you still see me as a home wrecker," Ashley said trying not to eye Jenna's ass as it jiggled as she walked from the bathroom to her bedroom.

"Girl,please. It ain't your fault that my husband ain't shit. It's my fault for knowing he wasn't shit and still saying, I do. Do you want something to eat or drink?"

Jenna strutted around naked like she was still the sexiest bitch at King's strip club as Ashley watched in confusion.

"Sure, I'll have some water."

"Okay, just let me throw on something and I'll get that for you. You can have a seat. Trust me, if I was going to do something, you would have been dead when you opened the front door."

Ashley sat on the couch while Jenna got dressed. Within seconds she walked out in a pair of boy shorts and a white tank top with no bra.

Ashley looked up and mumbled, "Damn."

Jenna replied, "Damn what? What's wrong?"

"Nothing, "Ashley replied with a smile, "I was just admiring how beautiful you are and wondering how much of a loser Tony had to be to fuck that up."

Jenna stared at her for a while with a bottle of Tequila in her hand before saying, "Thank you. Would you like to have a shot of this with me instead of water?"

"Yes, that's perfect," Ashley said while taking the Las Vegas themed shot glass from Jenna.

"Ashley, what do you like to do in your spare time?"

"Shop, shop, and shop," Ashley said, laughing.

"So, is that why y'all were in the mall?" She asked while refilling their shot glasses.

"Yes and No. I had a feeling he was hiding something because he never wanted to meet in public. It was more of a test to see if he would be the new member on my team but he failed."

"So you enjoyed the dick?"

"Huh?"

"The dick, Tony's dick. Did you enjoy him fucking you?"

"I... I don't feel comfortable answering that and maybe I should go." Ashley swallowed the shot like it was Kool-aid and grabbed her to stand but Jenna stood over her preventing her from getting up.

"No, I'm not ready for you to go yet. I'm enjoying your company and I promise you, I'm only asking because

I truly want to know. In a strange way, thinking about him putting his chunky long dick in you kind of turns me on."

Ashley unzipped her purse and pulled out her already rolled blunt and lighter then held it up.

"Do you mind? This shit here has me stressing?"

"Is it laced?"

"Hell nah, I'm a weed smoker and that's all I do besides drink. It helps me to do my thing on stage."

Jenna took the blunt out of her hand, lit it and pulled on it hard. When she released the smoke from her lungs she asked, "You strip too?"

"Yes, that's where I met Tony. Which club are you at?"

She hit the blunt again before answering and passing it, "He retired me. He said no wife of his would be shaking her ass for other men, but I was a headliner at King's. Now I work the front desk at the storage place on Washington and Crenshaw."

"I bet!" Ashley said hitting the blunt four times rapidly trying to fill her lungs to capacity to speed up the high. She couldn't deal with Jenna sober. "Can I have another shot, please?"

"Of course," she said and went to the kitchen to super-size their shot glasses with coffee mugs. "So, did you like Tony fucking you?"

Jenna wasn't into women, but the blunt and tequila didn't know it. It made her think about the way Ashley rubbed her back and the chills her touch sent down her spine she tried to ignore. As much as she tried to deny it the shit felt good especially since it had been weeks since Tony had touched her that way.

"No disrespect but yeah, the dick was good. He didn't last long, but I was enough to make me cum." The words came out of her mouth loose which let her know the weed was doing its job of relaxing her.

"Did you put those pretty lips on his dick, Ashley?"

"Only because he ate this pussy. Fair exchange no robbery!"

"Fair exchange, huh? Do you really think his whack ass head compared to what I'm sure your mouth can do was a fair exchange? I've never eaten pussy before, but I'm sure I can do better than his ass."

"What?" Ashley asked taken aback.

"You heard me."

Lost in the moment Jenna cuffed her face, kissed her, and Ashley openly accepted. She didn't stop the kiss because she was pissed at Tony for lying and putting her in this situation in the first place. The mother fucker was married and to a sexy bitch he probably could have talked into having a threesome instead of cheating and breaking her heart. Out of revenge she was willing to go as far as Jenna would let her.

Jenna felt her pussy being moistened by her juices. A woman had never made her feel this way before because she wasn't interested in given a woman the opportunity to try. Ashley took the blunt out of Jenna's hand, while they kissed and then broke their tongue by stepping back.

"Take them clothes back off." She hit the blunt as Jenna removed each piece like she was back on stage. Once she was stalk naked, Ashley used her unoccupied hand to cuff the fatty meat between Jenna's legs and allowed her fingers to rub against her clit. Jenna moaned in pleasure as she looked the woman in her eyes that her husband cheated with. She wanted her to suck on her pussy the way Ashley had sucked on her husband's dick.

"I'm Tony now, bitch. Suck mommy's clit until I cum in your nasty mouth, ho."

The words flowed out like she had said them before, and the strength in her voice made Ashley fall to her knees until her mouth met the pussy she wanted to taste in front of her.

Jenna raised her leg and rested it on the couch cushion.

She used her index and middle fingers to spread her pussy open to give access to her throbbing clit. Ashley looked up at Jenna and licked her lips.

"Put this pussy in your mouth, bitch."

She grabbed her by the back of her head rubbed her wet pussy all over her pretty face. *You ain't the only one cumming in Ashley's mouth, nigga.* Jenna thought as if Tony could hear her. The way Ashley had her mouth locked on Jenna's pussy would be like she was sucking a dick especially with Jenna pushing her head back and forth. Jenna felt superior and Ashley was now her bitch. She'd treat her however she wanted to.

This was the first time Jenna felt pleasure and pain at the same time. She grabbed Ashley by the hair and pushed her face deeper into her sweetness as she exploded on her bottom lip. She normally needed a break after orgasms that big but she hated Ashley and wanted to fill her throat up with her nuts like she was an elephant.

Ashley didn't mind the mistreatment by her lover either. She wanted to fuck Tony's wife better than he had ever done and then throw it in his face. Even if the couple did reconcile after all of this, Ashley wanted to be a fixture in both of their minds for the duration of the marriage because she was sure it wouldn't last long. They were too freaky for marriage and not freaky enough to fully satisfy each other. Ashley didn't know a thing about marriage counseling but she knew love, and it was absent from their relationship. The bond they had was built on lust and would be broken by the same source.

She rubbed her hand all over Jenna's soft ass gently while her tongue took its time exploring its surroundings. She knew exactly what her pussy wanted without Jenna having to say it. That was the beauty in a woman pleasing a woman; she was born with a cheat sheet.

"Suck my pussy harder. Make me cum,you freaky bitch!"

A part of Jenna wanted to beat the hell out of this whore while she ate her, but her curiosity was at its peak. *Was head from a woman always this good, or was Ashley putting on a show for?* She thought, while rotating her hips so her body matched the movement of the licks. Her lips whispered, "Stop!" but the juices from her pussy said different. Her thoughts were driving her crazy. Her heart was racing, juices flowing, and then,

"Ahhhhh....Fuck....Damn..." She exploded all over Ashley's face like she's never exploded before. She tightened her grip on Ashley's hair and snatched her face away from her pussy. She looked down at her while she tried to catch her breath and thought. *I don't even like this bitch, but she looks sexy as hell with my juices all over her face and those big brown eyes looking up at me for approval to keep sucking on my pussy.*

"Lick my pussy juices off your face and give me another kiss, bitch!"

Ashley stood up still looking her in the face, but she was moving too slowly for Jenna, so she licked her own juices off Ashley's lips, slapped the shit out her, and then seductively kissed her before Ashley assumed they were having a problem.

In response, Ashley grabbed her by the hand, led her to the bedroom, closed the door and then said, "Now I'm going to fuck you better than he's ever fucked you. Lay your pretty ass on the bed and open that pussy up. I want to see her."

Jenna wanted to ask her how she planned on doing that without a dick, but her pussy was begging to kiss Ashley's thick juicy lips again. She lied back on the bed and moaned as she pleasured herself with her fingers awaiting her mouth.

"Do you want this?" Ashley whispered in her ear as she kissed her lips, neck, and then the space between her breasts. "Do you want me to fuck that pussy better than that ho you married does?" She asked while she continued kissing her from her breast to her clit.

"Yes," Jenna moaned in pleasure, and then Ashley grabbed her trembling legs and spread them open. Her mouth watered at the sight of the way the juices ran down the crack of her ass to the comforter. She flicked her finger against her clit before slapping her pussy like she was giving it a high-five. The pain in the slap turned Jenna on even more.

"Taste me bitch, you're doing too much talking!" She moaned now holding her legs up in the air without help.

Ashley disciplined the pussy with another slap before spreading her lips and sucking on her clit. She looked up to make sure Jenna was enjoying every bit of it and she was as her eyes rolled back and the moans grew louder. Seconds before she was due to cum, Ashley stopped and stood up on the bed over her. She removed her clothes and then put herself in a scissor position on top of Jenna until their clits touch and the entrance to their lower mouths met. At first Jenna was skeptical that she's find pleasure in grinding their pussy's together, but the ecstasy came too quick for her to protest it.

Ashley rode her like she was sitting on a two inch dick, and for a second, Jenna thought she had grown one as she came back to back. The feeling was real, but penetration was missing in the action. Jenna managed to get Steve, her purple dildo that she kept hidden in space between her head board and mattress for night without Tony and nights she decided to fuck herself in front of him to show how useless he was to her.

"I need you to fuck the shit out of me," she yelled out.

Ashley wanting to give her exactly what she asked for slid the dildo into her juice box and went deep causing Jenna's body to shake uncontrollably and explode in multiple orgasms as she licked her pussy and blew on her asshole before sticking her thumb in it with the dildo in the other hand. Seeing Jenna come down from her orgasms made Ashley want to cause her another. She left the dildo inside of her and straddled her stomach. As she stroked in and out of Jenna, she rubbed her own clit on her stomach and forced her titty in her mouth. Surprisingly Jenna sucked on her nipple like it was attached to a bottle. They came together and Jenna went straight to sleep, drained.

Satisfied with what she'd done, Ashley grabbed her clothes and went into the bathroom. She rested her left leg on the rim of the bathtub and pleased herself until she came. This definitely wasn't what she expected when coming here and didn't really know what to think of it. She cleaned herself up, dressed, and walked out the adjoining door that led to the living room. She spotted the open bottle of patron on the table, took a swallow, grabbed her purse and keys, and walked out the door.

Jenna had only dosed off for a second and wanted to join Ashley in the shower for more, but she couldn't move.

Her clit was throbbing and her legs were still trembling. Tony had never devoured her pussy the way Ashley did. She wasn't sure if she'd dosed off again but she heard the front door close and was too exhausted to move. She hoped Ashley locked the door on her way out.

Jenna drifted off to sleep and was awakened a couple of hours later by loud music outside her bedroom window that she was sure came from Tony's car. Feeling guilty, she hopped up out of bed, threw on a big t-shirt, grabbed all the candles from the bathroom, put the Patron back into the kitchen cabinet, sat on the couch and turned on the TV.

"Hey, Jen, what did you do today?"

"I had company over. And you?"

"What company?" Tony asked.

"I think you gave up the right to ask me who, what, when, where, and why when you decided to cheat."

"No, I earned the right when I put that ring on your finger."

Jenna looked at her hand. "What ring? I don't see any rings."

"Jenna, where is your ring?" Tony asked. He was beginning to get irritated at her sarcasm.

"The same place yours is."

Tony waved his hand in front of Jenna's face. "My ring is right here."

Jenna laughed, "Well, I threw mine out the window somewhere on Slauson."

"You threw a two-carat ring out the fucking window? Jenna, you're a dumb bitch."

"I wasn't dumb enough for you to marry," Jenna replied, trying her hardest not to let him see her tearing up.

"Yeah and that's the reason I'm doing the shit I do," he said, sarcastically.

"Anything you can do, I can do better," Jenna mumbled, wiping the tears from her eyes.

Tony stood at the foot of bed and replied

angrily,"What the hell is that supposed to mean?"

Jenna threw him a blanket and said,

"Sleep on it. Hopefully, your dumb ass will figure it out by morning."

"And you left your company in bed," he said throwing the dildo out the bedroom door to the living. "Now the bed smells like pussy and plastic," he finished with a laugh at how pathetic she was.

The phone rang and Jenna picked it up on the first ring.

"Hello!" she yelled into the phone.

"Hey, sexy, what are you doing?"

"Getting ready for bed and you?"

"Sitting here thinking about you."

"Who is this?" Jenna asked already knowing the answer.

"It's me, Ashley."

"How did you get my number?"

"I was thinking about you on my ride home, and it

came to me Tony never texted me from his friend's phone, so it mus had to have been you," she giggled.

Damn, I forget to change my number after I texted that bitch. Jenna thought and then said, "Well, Ashley, I'll leave you to think of me while I get some sleep. I have a busy day tomorrow."

"Sleep tight. Don't let the boogie man bite," Ashley replied.

"He won't," Jenna said, laughing. "Goodnight, Ashley."

Jenna woke up to the sound of slamming doors and drawers. She got up and looked in the kitchen. Tony was cleaning the mess Jenna had left the night before. She started to say thank you, but for what? He didn't work, so shit, he needed to clean up. On the other hand, Jenna did work so she dressed and went there. There were two dozen roses on her desk when she got there. Jenna smiled. *Tony trying to get me to forgive him.* She thought. She read the card:

I can't wait to taste that candy apple again. Don't keep me waiting long!

Ashley

Candy apple? Jenna thought. She never heard anyone call it that before. She spent all day at her desk thinking about how good it felt to be touched by Ashley and how she could get used to it as long as she didn't have to return the favor. She decided to call Ashley.

"This is Ashley."

"Hey. Do you want to meet up for lunch?"

"Sure, Jenna. Where do you want to go?"

"I'm close to the Crenshaw Mall is that okay with you?"

"Yes, I'm already up here. Had to exchange some shoes."

"Okay, I'll see you in a few," Jenna said.

Toya kept calling, but Jenna sent her to voicemail so

she sent her a text instead.

Bitch, I know you see my calls. I'm waiting to hear all the details about you and Ashy. Call me back!

Jenna didn't know what she was going to tell Toya, but whatever she told her, it sure wouldn't be the truth. Jenna stepped out of the car in her purple, mini dress and black heels. Ashley met her at the food court.

"So how is your day going?" Ashley asked.

"So far, so good. I don't have any complaints and yours?"

"I'm having a wonderful day. Seeing you in that dress has made it 10 times better."

Jenna smiled.

"I have something for you." Ashley pulled out a small envelope.

"What's this?"

"Just a little something to say thank you."

"Thank you for what?" Jenna asked.

41

"For being you! You could have pulled a crazy bitch move on me for what happened but instead you let me umm… you let me get to know you," Ashley responded, with a smile.

"Thank you how sweet." Jenna opened the envelope. It was a gift card for a hundred dollars to Victoria's Secret. Jenna handed it back to Ashley.

"I can't accept this." Ashley pushed it back.

"Yes, you can. You just did. I want to see you in something Tony hasn't."

After eating, they went their separate ways promising to call each other that night. Jenna let the night pass without calling Ashley. She didn't know how she felt about her and wasn't ready to have a heart to heart about it. She continued to ignore Toya's calls, too.

The next morning on her ride to work, Jenna was sitting at the stop light when a Tahoe pulled up next to her.

"Excuse me, beautiful. Would you mind giving me

your number so I can get to know you better?"

Normally, Jenna would ignore it, but just to spite Tony, she exchanged numbers with him. Ronald or so he claimed that was his name was brown-skin, tall, with a medium build from what she could tell with him sitting in his truck which was just how she liked them. She could tell he had nipple rings because she could see them through his shirt.

"I will call you in an hour," Ronald said.

"Okay," Jenna responded, before taking off. Jenna called Toya.

"Hey, girl, what are you up to?"

"I was about to text you and curse you out. When were you going to call me with the details?"

"I was; I just needed to figure out what to tell you."

"Okay, now you gon' make me come over there," Toya said, laughing.

"No, it's cool," Jenna said, laughing with her.

"Hold on. Before you start, I might need a drink for this."

Toya sat the phone down, poured herself a cup of coffee and continued her conversation. "Okay, girl, I'm back."

"I invited her over and she popped up while I was in the bath so she came in and she told me that she met Tony in a club. He was with two other guys as he approached her."

"It had to be Alex and Donald with him," Toya said with certainty. "They go everywhere together."

"I figured it was them, too," Jenna lied.

"She said they have been talking for about three months and have had sex six to eight times. Once at my house and the rest were at her house. All it took was a couple shots of Patron for her to start telling it all."

"What the hell? He had the nerve to bring that bitch in your house and sex her? That is a trifling ass man," Toya yelled into the phone. "I am livid, Jen, and he isn't even my man. You deserve so much more."

"I'm not even tripping, T, because she came into my house and I let her taste the candy apple as she calls it."

"Wait; come again," Toya said, confused.

"I wasn't going to tell you at first, but I have to tell someone. I said I let her taste the candy apple as she calls it."

"One more time," Toya said, wanting to be sure she heard her.

"The bitch ate me out; is that better?" Jenna laughed.

"What the hell? When the hell did you become gay, Jen?"

"I'm not gay!"

"Yes, you are!" Toya yelled.

"Well, shit, I was for one night. We had Patron, and she kissed me and I figured that would be the best revenge."

"Oh my," Toya said.

"Oh my, what?" Jenna replied laughing.

"You got turned out. That's what." Toya was on the other end of the phone in shock. She didn't know what was about to come out of Jenna's mouth.

"It's cool," Jenna continued. "I had my eyes closed pretending she was my dream man. Sis, she touched me like no man ever has before."

"You are off the chain for that one, Jenna. Where was Tony while all of this was going on?"

"At his mother's house."

"Jenna, what would you have donep if he had walked in?"

"Nothing; let him watch," Jenna snickered.

"Now that would have been a scene."

"We went to lunch yesterday, and she gave me a gift card for a hundred dollars to Victoria's Secret."

"So, basically, she's a trick."

"Yes, basically, but who cares? If she likes it, I love it."

"You better be careful before you get into some shit you didn't ask for."

"Shit like what?" Jenna asked.

"Like a stalker. What if she starts to like you more than she likes Tony?"

"Oh, well, that will be his bad and hers, too, because I met this fine ass dude on my way to work. I don't want to know shit about him but my pussy do."

"You are really outdoing yourself, Jenna," she said while thinking and shaking her head. *This girl is crazy.*

"I sure am and why not, Tony is? And besides, was Tony thinking of me when he sexed Ashley and all those other bitches? No, and I'm sure he isn't thinking of me now," Jenna said angrily. "I even told him when we were arguing that when I find a fine ass man we can double date."

"You are a fool and want to die. I'm laughing my ass off at you not with you, Jen."

"Toya, I'm at work. You have the scoop now, so call me later."

"Okay, sis, I have to marinate all this info. Talk to you later, bye."

Before Jenna could put the office phone down, her cell rang.

"Hello."

"Good morning. May I speak with Jenna?"

"Speaking; who's calling?"

"This is Ronald."

"Oh. Good morning, Ronald. How are you?"

"I'm blessed, but need to see you out of traffic."

"Is that right?"

"Yeah, I was actually calling to see if you wanted to join me for breakfast if you're not at work?"

"I'm at work but I can get away. When and where do

you want to meet?"

"The IHOP on Crenshaw. I will be there in about an hour."

"Okay, let me get someone to cover this desk, and I'll be there."

"Okay. See you in a minute, beautiful."

Jenna hopped up, headed for the door, and was met by Tony.

"Where are you going in a rush?" Tony asked, dressed to impress, and smelling good. He had heart to heart and realized that he was fucking up a good thing. It was time to get his marriage back tight.

"To drop Toya off at the airport; I'm running late. I got to go..."

"I was hoping we could go to breakfast or something. I want to make it up to you baby. I'm sorry!"

"I don't know about all that, but how about trying to make it up over dinner? I got to go!" She jumped in the car and left Tony standing there looking stupid.

Jenna pulled up to IHOP and was seated with Ronald who was already waiting.

"Hi, beautiful. How are you?"

Jenna was so focused on how large the muscles in his arms were that she barely heard what he said.

"Hey," she responded dumbfounded, with a smile.

He chuckled realizing he had her in a daze and then said, "What do want to eat and don't say me. I'm not on the menu."

"Then I'm not hungry; I just came to see you."

"Okay, well. I can order my food a little later then."

Jenna and Ronald sat there for hours flirting, talking about their past relationships and the one Jenna was about to get out of. Ronald had asked questions no man had ever asked her like, what she wanted out of life and what was she doing to brighten her future. Caught off guard she searched the room for an answer instead of racking her, and then something told Jenna to look out the window. Ashley was getting out of the passenger side of Tony's car and although they were walking up together, neither looked interested in being in the other's company. *Must be trouble in paradise.* Jenna thought while shaking her head.

"Speaking of the devil," she said to Ronald before he could ask her what was wrong. She cut her eyes toward Tony.

Ronald looked toward the door while taking a sip of water.

"Wait; is that your husband walking in now and holding another chick's hand?"

"Yep, that's the same chick I caught him with, and they both told me they were done with each other," Jenna responded.

"What are you going to do?"

"Nothing, continue to enjoy my time with you."

Tony and Ashley were seated and talking to their

waitress when Tony noticed Jenna laughing at the table across the room with another nigga.

"Excuse me,babe. I'll be right back," Tony said walking toward his wife and her side piece.

Jenna grabbed Ronald's hand when she noticed Tony headed their way.

"Aye, homie. Who are you?" Tony asked aggressively.

"I'm Ronald, and you are?" He replied with a smirk. "Is there a problem?"

"Hell yeah!" It's a problem, nigga. That's my wife."

"By the looks of it, y'all put that whole marriage shit on time, or did you forget that you walked in here with a bitch." Ronald stood up and looked Tony in his face sideways. "Either you handle your problem or you step."

Jenna jumped up from her seat.

"No, y'all are not going to do this here. Ronald, please sit down." She turned to face Tony, "You came in here with the same bitch from the mall you claim you're not fucking but in my face like I'm wrong. Boy bye?!"

Tony never took his eyes off Ronald as he raised his hand to hit Jenna but Ronald reached over the table and punched him in the face before Tony's fist could connect. Tony stumbled backward into the person behind him. Ashley watched from a far until the hit sent her running over to the table and grabbed Tony. Ashley tried to pull him away from the table before he could hit Ronald back. Jenna managed to get Ronald outside and into the parking lot while the manager and Ashley held Tony inside.

"Why did you hit him?"

"Fuck that nigga. You don't step to a man like that and think shit ain't gone happen. I'm a fucking man, Jenna, not a little bitch your husband can run up on. So you might want to go back in there and make sure your husband is straight. I'll get at you later."

Ronald hopped in his car and drove off.

Jenna was upset and didn't want things with Ronald to end like this before they even started. For a split second she debated which man to run after and decided to get in her car and follow Ronald. Two hours of talking with him was worth more than the wasted years with Tony. She caught up to Ronald at a stop light and motioned for him to roll his window down.

"Ronald can you please pull over. I know you saw me behind you. Just for a minute, please!"

Hesitating for a second, Ronald decided to pull over and walked up to Jenna's window.

"Yeah what's up?"

"I'm sorry about all of that. I didn't know he was planning on eating there. I don't want things to end like that before they even begin. Let's just go somewhere and finish our date. Please?"

"If that's what you really want to do, get in your car and follow me."

Ronald and Jenna spent the entire day together laughing and joking. They walked on the beach and went to the pier. Jenna had a good time and could see herself in a relationship with Ronald. He didn't mention IHOP or Tony as if it never happened. When they made it to his house, she felt like she was at home.

"First, I want to know if I can suck on these," Jenna asked, while running her fingertips across his chest. "I have a nipple fetish and yours are sexy as fuck with the rings in them."

"Okay, but I'm not responsible for what may happen after you do that," Ronald said, seductively.

And I'm not responsible if my lips end up sucking on something else. Jenna thought.

Jenna only stood five-foot, one, which put her lips right at his nipples when they hugged. She gently sucked on his nipples and nibbled around them. Ronald's dick grew harder and harder. She put her hands in his pants to see what he was working with. *Nice and thick.* She thought.

"See what you did?" Ronald said, pointing to his pants.

Kissing and rubbing on him, Jenna answered, "Yes."

"Well, too bad because today isn't the day you're going to get it. I don't fuck on the first date," Ronald said, pulling away from her.

Jenna laughed. "It's cool because I don't either."

After flirting and teasing all the way to her car, they bypassed it and were in his truck, fucking. Jenna rode his dick until her pussy juices covered his lap and dripped to his leather seats. Ronald shot his nut in her like pregnancy was obsolete.

Jenna walked in from her date to find Tony and Ashley on the couch kissing. She walked past them as if they didn't exist. Tony almost peed in his pants when he heard the bedroom door slam. Jenna could take a lot but not seeing that. She picked up the phone, called Ronald, and asked him if she could come over. "Sure," he said, so she grabbed a change of clothes, threw them in a bag, and headed out the door, making sure to stop and whisper in Tony's ear,

"How do you like tasting my candy apple every time you kiss her?"

Tony stood up and walked to the door and yelled,

"What the fuck did you just say to me?"

Jenna stopped in her tracks, looked back and yelled,

"You heard me and if not, ask Ashley what I said."

Tony slammed the door in anger.

"What the hell did she mean by that, Ashley?"

"Mean by what?" Ashley said confused.

"Don't fucking play with me," he said, grabbing Ashley by the arm, "Bitch, that is my wife, and I'm not fucking playing when it comes to her!"

"Wait, say that again," Ashley cried.

Tony just looked at her. He wanted to believe Jenna was just fucking with his head, but the rage he was feeling wouldn't allow him to let it go. Tony paced the floor trying to calm down.

"Ashley, she's my wife."

"Remember, you never told me you were married, Tony.

Tony replied, "I just did."

Ashley slapped him and he grabbed her by the throat.

"Bitch, don't you ever put your fucking hands on me."

"You don't know me like that!" Ashley screamed out as she stared at him in awe. "I can't believe you put your hands on me."

"And I can't believe you fucked my wife!"

"I could say the same to you. You told me you were single for life. What happened to that shit? You lied to me!"

"Bitch, I don't owe you the truth!" He yelled.

"Oh, okay, I see what the problem is," Ashley said, looking around for her purse. "You can fuck around on your wife, but anybody that touches the candy apple gets fucked up?" Ashley said.

"You damn right, bitch."

"Well I only have four words for you," she said grabbing her purse and keys. "Her pussy was good!" Ashley stopped at the door and looked back at Tony. "I don't know what type of bitches you're used to fucking with, but they ain't me. The next time you even think about putting your hands on me, I will blast yo' ass. Don't let the look fool you. I may be just as hard if not harder than your broke ass. Take some advice," she said opening the door. "Get up, dust yourself off, find a job, and treat your wife the way she deserves to be treated. I would hate to have to take her from you."

Ashley walked off, leaving the door open and Tony's face hanging to the floor.

"Jenna?" Ashley said surprised that Jenna answered her.

"What?!"

Ashley began talking, but Jenna wasn't listening. She took the phone from her to tell Ronald.

"This bitch," Jenna said to Ronald.

"What, bitch?" He asked curiously.

"The bitch, Ashley that Tony was with at IHOP." She put the phone back to her ear.

"Look Ashley, I really didn't want you to get involved, but you did that all on your own."

"Are you serious Jenna? I never asked you to kiss me?"

"No, you didn't, but you didn't say no, either."

"Jenna, you were begging me eat the pussy."

"I just needed to know how long he had been fucking with you. If you were me, you would want to know, too."

"You're right; I would," Ashley agreed. "But I wouldn't go about it the way you did. I would simply have asked the bitch if she was fuckin' my husband."

"You're right and I apologize. Is there any way I can

make it up to you?"

"Yeah, you can let me taste that candy apple again."

"I wasn't talking about in that way," Jenna said, looking up at Ronald as if he could hear Ashley.

"Well, you asked. Can you come over? I'm not trying to sleep with you, but I do want to tell you how I ended up with your husband at IHOP and what happened after you left us at the apartment."

"What happened when I left?" Jenna was curious but didn't want Ronald to know what was going on. "Text me your address and I'll be there in a couple of hours. I'm sorry you were dragged into this."

"I don't understand why you are apologizing to her when she was fucking your husband?" Robert asked when she hung up the phone feeling more confused than he was this morning.

"I know you don't understand and I promise I will explain everything to you later. I really need to handle this right now before it gets out of hand."

"Do what you need to do, Jen; I'm only a phone call away."

Ronald walked Jenna to the door, hugged her goodbye. *Women.* He thought as he watched her drive away.

Jenna nervously knocked on Ashley's door. She didn't know what to expect. Ashley opened the door and looked Jenna up and down.

"So I see you decided to wear pants today."

"Yes, it's cold outside," Jenna answered with sarcasm.

"I love the way your ass is looking in them jeans and heels," Ashley said looking Jenna up and down.

"Look, I only came over to find out what happened when I left. I'm not here for anything else!" Jenna rolled her eyes in frustration.

"You're acting like you don't want to be here, and if that's the case, you can leave."

"It's not that, Ashley. I've never been with a woman

before and I will admit I haven't been able to get you out of my mind. I want to forget about what happened between us but I can't. I want to hate you for fucking with my husband, but my pussy jumped when I saw y'all kissing on my couch. Hell, a part of me wished you were kissing me on the couch. I'm not gay but you're making me feel like I am.

Jenna heard a noise outside Ashley's door and froze, "Do you think Tony will popping up?"

"No, I don't think he will be coming here ever again. I let his ass have it."

"What happened?"

"That asshole put his hands on me. I walked away this time; next time, he won't be walking, period." She said as ringing interrupted her building again. "Is that your cell ringing? It isn't mine."

Jenna pulled her cell from her purse. *Damn, Tony, not now.* She thought.

"Hello?"

"Where in the fuck are you?"

"Tony, I told you before; you gave up the right to ask me anything about my personal life when you decided to fuck other people and not give a fuck about bringing them in front of me."

"Jenna, I know I was wrong, but why did you have to do me like that?"

"Do you like what, Tony?"

"Why you let that bitch lick yo' shit?"

"The same reason you fucked her, she wanted to and it felt good."

"I got something for both you bitches!"

Tony slammed the phone down and finished off Jenna's bottle of Patron. The more he thought of Ashley between his wife's legs the more enraged he became. The Patron made him feel untouchable and he began throwing punches at the air pretending he was fighting Ronald and Ashley at the same time. He was delusional and even went as far as pulling out his dick and spraying the couch with his pee. In his feeble mind he thought he was peeing on both of his enemies' dead bodies. After knocking holes in the walls and breaking everything he had paid for in their apartment, Tony hopped in his truck and drove off.

"Oh, well, I guess he hung up," Jenna said, laughing.

"Well, since it felt so good,,Jen; why not let me finish what I started? You know he doesn't know you're over here if he's calling."

"You know what? I'm not gay, nor do I like girls!" Jenna snapped. "I do like my pussy ate but by men. I only did it to get back at Tony. Why don't you understand that?"

"Because, that's real fucked up! How could you lead me on like that? You just said you were craving me!" Ashley cried.

Jenna felt bad for doing what she did. She never wanted to hurt Ashley and believed she hadn't known about her in the beginning, but Ashley was a damn fool to forget that hours ago she was back at their apartment kissing her husband on her couch.

"I'll tell you what," Jenna said wiping the tears from Ashley's face. "I won't beat your ass for making out with my husband after you knew about me if you promise to leave me the fuck alone. Yeah, you did eat the hell out of my pussy, but you're a ho and I don't do bitches!'

"Is that right?" Ashley said as she walked towards her couch. Jenna didn't like how she said it and wasn't sure if she could run out fast enough if Ashley was going for a gun. She didn't know what to do but quickly decided to sip game.

"We can make a deal. You can have me as much as you want as long as I don't have to return the favor. I'm not eating any pussy, but I will suck on those pretty titties you have. Is that a deal?"

Ashley sniffled. A smile grew on her face, and she began walking back towards Jenna. "I will take what I can get, baby."

"On second thought, we had better not, not right now. Let me go end things with Ronald and Tony. Then you can have me to yourself until I find the right man," Jenna said, walking toward the door.

"I guess this is goodbye for now then, but can I have a kiss before you go?"

"This isn't goodbye, baby. It's a see you later and you can have more than a kiss when I get back." Jenna blew her a kiss with no plans of seeing the crazy bitch again and then closed the door behind her.

Jenna started her car and pulled off. Tony, who was parked down the street, spotted Jenna leaving Ashley's house.

"That bitch still fucking with my wife?!" Tony yelled as he slammed his fist on the dashboard.

Jenna sent Ronald a text saying she was on her way to get in bed with him and he encouraged the sleep over. She pulled up to Ronald's house with food for the two of them and told him about everything that happened between her and Ashley. Ronald was shocked, but now he understood.

"Baby, let me take care of you," he said, sliding her heels off and massaging her feet. "There ain't a bitch or nigga on this planet that can do you like Big Ron. I don't want anything in return from you. It sounds like you have given the wrong motherfuckas too much already, and it's time to receive. Tell big Ron what you want?"

"Big Ron, huh? Ok, first I want you to kiss me on my neck and keep going down to the middle of my back." Ronald did as he was told.

Damn, this is feeling good. I'm going to release before he even gets inside of me, she thought.

"It's my turn to call the shots," he announced as he turned Jenna over and kissed her while cupping a hand full of her pussy through her pants. When he felt it warm up, he unbutton her pants and let his fingers play in her moisture.

Whenever he felt his fingers fully coated he wiped them off with his tongue as she watched.

"Fuck that. Put your tongue in it!" She moaned and grabbed his head, guiding him to her sweet spot. Just as he kissed the inside of her thigh, her phone rang.

Now my phone is ringing. Fuck. She thought as she reached her hand down into her purse to cut it off but the name that came up made her decide to answer it.

"Hello?"

"Jenna, Tony is all over the news."

"For what?" Jenna said, pushing Ronald's mouth away from her pussy and sitting up. She could hear the panic in Toya's voice.

"That girl, Ashley got shot and from what the neighbors are telling the news anchor. They saw a woman leave the apartment and shortly after, she let a man in named Tony. He must have been there a lot for them to know his name, face and truck."

"Oh, my GOD! He saw me," Jenna yelled, slipping back into her pants.

"What's going on now?" Ronald asked putting on his shoes.

"I don't know yet, hold on," Jenna answered as her best friend kept talking.

"The neighbors heard arguing and gun shots firing, and when the police got there, her front door was open and she was lying in a pool of blood."

"Why did he...Okay...I have to find him, " Jenna cried, uncontrollably while putting on her shoes.

"I'll call you back, Toya."

"Baby, are you okay?" Ronald asked concerned.

"No, I have to go find Tony!"

Jenna grabbed her shoes, purse, and car keys and ran out the door.

After following his wife to buy food to feed another nigga he watched her pull into Ronald house and then drove off. If wasn't positive if it was his house or not but when he put the address in Google, Ronald Jones came up as the owner. He wanted to spray up the place to scare Jenna and send Ronald a message, but he didn't own a gun and he had a bitch he needed to handle first. Once he convinced Ashley to let him in, her mouth and the disrespectful words she let out of it forced him to beat her until she was sleep. Seeing the gun she tried to hide under her shirt is what made him take it and finish her off. In his mind, it was self defense, and the Patron acted as his lawyer convincing him that it was self-defense. Now with a gun in hand and only three bullets left in it, he slowly drove past Ronald's house before parking at the corner.

So this nigga thinks he can fuck my wife and put hands on me. Tony thought and then planned on waiting until 4 am and putting all three bullets in Ronald as Jenna watched, but an hour and a half later he looked up to see Jenna leaving his house.

Unable to control his anger, he pulled his black hoodie over his head, exited the car, and walked five houses down to Ronald's door. His adrenaline raced as rang the doorbell.

Good she changed her mind. Ronald thought as his dick jumped while opening the door. Standing there, face to face with him was Tony with a gun in hand...

"Please go back to Ronald's house," Toya pleaded with Jenna when she called her to say she'd be out looking for her husband. "What if he shoots your ass next?"

"He's not going to shoot me. He loves me and I love him. This shit has gone too far. I'm about to get my husband and drive straight to Mexico. We will start over there and when we get straight, you can come visit, okay?"

Toya could hear the fear in her best friend's voice but wouldn't hold back her thoughts. She loved the girl since they were knee high, but she couldn't lie to her and make everything sound like it will be alright.

"Bitch are you crazy? This nigga is on one. At least

wait until tomorrow sis and see if he reaches out to you, please? I'm going to my aunt's house in Northridge because we both know that nigga is going to come by here looking for you!"

Tired of hearing Toya's mouth and starting to feel there was some truth to what she was saying, she agreed and headed back to Ronald's.

Turning the corner to his block, the streets were blocked off and there were police and paramedics everywhere. Jenna got out the car and walked up to the front of the crowd gathered in the street. She screamed in horror as she watched the paramedics roll Ronald out on a stretcher with a blood sheet covering his body.

The End

THE PENSTRESS

Twix

Sitting back appreciating the relationship between us as it grows each day. Not wanting to ruin the friendship with these few grown up words I'm about to say.

Do you remember the short walks and talks we had? The smile and nod I took as the go ahead from your dad?

Our families have always been too close for us to start anything. I'm like fuck that though, ain't neither one of us wearing a ring.

You keep saying, "The time isn't now but it may come soon." I'll make you eat them words if I can get you into my room.

This friendship shit, yeah, it's cool so I've been playing a long.All the while waiting to show you how it spreads when I come up out this thong.

Boy, when are you gone come fuck Ms. Parker? Ironically that's my last name, I'm trying to swallow your first born son and daughter.

I'm more than a good friend, cute face, and figure full of curves. You'd know this by now if I could get up the nerve.

Here, sit down for a minute let me give it a few tries. I'm mean, why not, I've been fucking since you walked in with eyes.

If I had one night with you I'd keep it to myself. Relax, get comfortable let me help you get rid of that belt.

I know a little Hennessey and Kush will get that dick on the rise. My self-esteem is intact, you can blame fucking me on being drunk or high.

Inebriation can't ruin the first time and this sure isn't going to be the last. Spread both of those cheeks apart, I want my clit licked but you can end in my ass.

Got me biting on my lip, thinking about Mr. Goodbar's tongue on my clit. Umm, a double scoop of chocolate and caramel, might as well call you my Twix.

Oops is that a finger, baby? you can put that away, yeah you can stop. You don't need help this pussy wet, dripping and you know that monkey hot.

Guess I'll stop here because this won't be quick but I swear on our bond I'll have you thinking about the different ways I rode your dick!

THE PENSTRESS

Red Hot

Waking up from a long night out with the girls Alicia headed to the kitchen for a glass of water.

"I'm going out for a while with mama. I'll be back later. Maurice is out back and the kids are gone," Tamika yelled from the living room when she heard the sound of someone using the water dispenser on the refrigerator. "And make sure you leave your cell on just in case I can't get back in. I lost my keys."

"I got you T, I will be here all day" Alicia responded. "If I do decide to leave I'll let you know and where are you and mama going?"

"Don't play! You already know mama wasn't missing out on that70% off sale. She's been blowing the horn trying to rush me out the house like the store is about to shut down. Let Maurice know that I left, please."

"I will."

Alicia laid out her clothes, put on her slow jams CD, and got into the shower. Singing along to Piece of my Love by Guy she didn't notice Maurice walk in. He took his clothes off and slid the shower curtain back startling her.

"Boy, don't play like that. You scared me!"

"I saw Tamika pull off." He said kissing her neck and groping her wet breast.

"The kids might come in and find us," Alicia said cautiously.

"No they won't they're gone for the summer."

Maurice pulled Alicia closer to him ensuring she felt his hardness on her butt. He turned her around and kissed her sloppily. She took Maurice's hand and touched her stomach with it.

"I'm pregnant, Big Daddy."

He pretended not to hear her; cut the water off got out the shower and went into his daughter's room. Alicia grabbed a towel and followed him not knowing what he was thinking after her declaration. Maurice turned the music up, locked the door behind her and got on his knees. He rubbed and kissed her stomach.

"Don't worry we will figure this out" he said while getting off his knees and leading her to the twin covered in teddy bears he had won at different amusement parks for his princess over the years.

Alicia knew the routine and laid back on the bed dodging the stuffed animals. He took her legs placed them on his shoulders and entered her deep but all Alicia could think about was how her sister would react when she found out she was pregnant by her husband. After the months of orgasming on her brother in-law's dick while her sister ran errands, guilt had final visited her. She couldn't look Maurice in the face. She slid down on his dick, flipped her legs over and took his drilling on all four. Maurice slapped her on her ass in excitement.

He must love me and want the baby, Alicia thought. Look at how he's fucking me.

After an hour of shopping with her mother, which had to be to the fastest shopping experience she'd encounter with her, Tamika walked into the house to find the music blasting. She headed straight for her son's room but she remembered he wasn't home to irk her nerves so the music wasn't coming from there. She followed the sound to her daughter's room, only to find her door was locked. Raven never locked her door, she thought. Tamika grabbed the spare key from under her mattress and unlocked the door. She was shocked to see two people having sex like dogs in the space she kissed her baby good night. What was even more shocking was the fact that they hadn't noticed her opening the door. Tamika stood there waiting to see if they would notice her. When they hadn't she flicked on the lights only to see her husband's dick coming out of her sister's wet box raw. In tears, Tamika ran to the kitchen. Maurice chased after her while Alicia stayed in the room throwing her clothes on. He caught up to her and held her tight. It took lots of energy but she was able to snatch away from him and grab the knife that was lying on the counter. He started to back up. She wanted to laugh seeing him standing there scared to death with nothing on but socks but the now white coating of her sister's juices drying on his shrunken dick kept her anger where it needed to be.

Alicia walked out the bedroom and toward the kitchen. She could see Tamika had Maurice backed against the kitchen sink. As kids, Alicia would call her sister Red Hot, whenever she was mad because she was light skin and her face would turn pink when bothered. Pink was mild to the red she was seeing in her sister's face.

"Please Tamika," he begged.

"Please what? Please don't kill you, please let you put on some clothes, or is it please let me finish fucking your sister?"

Alicia stood in the hallway hoping not to be seen by Tamika.

"No baby please let me explain."

"Please let you explain? No explanations needed. You had your shriveled little dick inside my sisters cob webbed pussy. I am a grown ass woman. I know exactly how that happens."

Alicia tried to tip toe to the front door. She put her hand on the knob and twisted it.

"Naw, little bitch, where in the fuck do you think you're going?"

Alicia turned toward her.

"I wasn't leaving."

"Sit your ass down. Your ass wasn't trying to leave before I got here."

Alicia shaking sat down on the couch. She could see the fear in Maurice's eyes. She slipped her hand into her pocket and dialed 9-1-1just in case Tamika got to tripping.

Tamika looked at Alicia then at Maurice. Then she took the knife that was in her hands and sliced her wrist. Maurice ran to her and took the knife. Alicia sent the call to the police and ran to her sister to put pressure on her wrist with the towel she grabbed from the counter. Tamika started to pass in and out of consciousness. Blood was everywhere. When the paramedics arrived, Maurice was in the room dressing. By the time he came out of the room, the police had Alicia in handcuffs. He started walking toward Alicia but the police handcuffed him too. Yelling

Maurice said, "Why are we in handcuffs if she cut herself?"

"Sir, until we can get this all situated we have to take you both down for questioning."

"Did she say we did this?"

"Sir, she hasn't said anything."

"Well, why are you taking us?" Maurice yelled the words at the officer.

"Just get in the car and let us sort all this out. The longer you sit here and argue with me, the longer it's going to be before you can come back home."

Later that night at the hospital, Tamika woke up to detectives standing over her ready to begin their questioning about what happened.

"Tamika, I'm Detective Vargas and this is Detective Ray. Do you know why you're in the hospital?"

"Yes. My wrist was cut."

"How did that happen?"

It took Tamika about five minutes to answer.

"I came home from shopping with my mother and went to my daughter's room to turn off the radio. When I opened the door, I saw my sister having sex with my husband. She got up and went to the bathroom and Maurice ran toward the kitchen. I ran after him yelling and screaming and crying and he grabbed a knife from the drawer."

Tamika started to cry.

"I'm sorry mam', this won't take long." The visibly youngest detective in the room announced and Tamika continued as if she had never stopped.

"I tried to run toward the living room to get away and my sister was in the way. So I begged her to let me out the door and she said no let's talk about this. I said I didn't want to talk I wanted to leave. I pushed pass her and that's when Maurice grabbed my arm. He mumbled something about being in love with my sister and suicide. When I heard it, I tried to snatch away but he was holding me too tight and then he cut my wrist with the knife. I remember falling to the ground and nothing after that."

"When we got there your sister was holding your wrist trying to stop the bleeding and the knife was in her hands. Your husband was in the bedroom getting dressed. Do you remember if you sister said anything to you while you were on the floor?"

"No. I don't."

Tamika closed her eyes weak from all the blood she had lost. Back at the police station Maurice was trying to convince detectives that Tamika cut herself.

"Man, I was naked and she had me backed against the

sink. She pointed the knife toward me then cut herself. After that, Alicia grabbed the knife and tried to stop the bleeding. I will take a lie detector test if I have to. I'm sure Alicia will tell you the same thing."

"Alicia, Maurice already told us that you cut Tamika. So now it's time for you to tell us the truth."

"He said what?" Alicia screamed pounding her fists in her hands. Crying she said, "I love my sister. Yeah, I slept with her husband but I love her. All I tried to do was stop the bleeding. She had Maurice against the kitchen sink and she was getting ready to cut him then she turned the knife on herself. I grabbed the knife so she wouldn't cut herself anywhere else. When I applied pressure, she passed out. Ask her. She will tell you."

"We already asked her and she said you held her down while Maurice cut her." Pissed Alicia sat down.

"Give all of us a lie detector test. She's lying and I

want a lawyer."

Two hours later Alicia and Maurice were booked for attempted murder. Tamika was released from the hospital three days later.

"Thank you Reka for picking me up."

"Who else would come get your crazy ass?"

"My mom," Tamika said smiling.

"Girl, I can't believe that they were in your house in your baby's bed."

"Reka, I tried to kill his ass, but I couldn't so I cut myself and told the police they did it.

"Do you know your ass could go to jail for that?" Reka asked.

"Yes, but they are going to pay one way or the other. It will be worth it to see them suffer."

"Damn, T, and you're always telling me to do the right thing."

"Fuck them they can go to hell," Tamika said with anger in her voice.

Reka pulled up to Tamika's house. They were amazed to see how much blood was still on the kitchen floor. You could see all the places where the police took fingerprints. Tamika looked at Reka and started crying.

"Don't cry T,"Reka said hugging her. "It's gonna be okay."

"I know," Tamika mumbled.

"Come on. I'll help you clean this mess up. We have two hours to do it because I have to get my mom's car back by six."

An hour later, Reka hugged Tamika goodbye and left. The following day Reka took the bus to work just as she usually did. As usual, the bus was packed standing room only. Reka looked around trying to find a seat. The only seat she saw was next to the same guy she saw on the bus the other day. Reka pretended not to see the seat but he smiled and tapped her on the leg.

"There's an empty seat right here if you want it." He smiled.

"Sure thanks." Feeling like she should say something she said, "Every time I see you you're smiling."

"Well, that's because you give me a reason to smile."

Reka rolled her eyes.

"Whatever."

"No it's true. You're beautiful." His smile grew at the relief of confessing.

"Thank you."

"You can thank me with your number so I can take you out sometimes."

"If I had met you anywhere but here I would but I don't date guys that ride the bus."

He fell out laughing.

"How shallow is that?"

"Not shallow at all. It's just a preference."

"Wow," he said in amazement.

"You know, with preferences like that it's going to be hard for you to find anyone at all."

Reka was getting mad.

"No, not hard at all."

"Okay, if you say so pretty lady. This is my stop. You enjoy the rest of your ride."

"Thank you. I will," Reka said sarcastically. She

looked out the window as the bus pulled off. She was surprised to see him walk into the Mercedes dealership.

"Hmmm," she thought. "I should have gotten that number after all".

After work, Reka rushed in the house to call Tamika and tell her about the guy she met on the bus. However, to her surprise Tamika was at her house sitting at the kitchen table.

"Hey, when did you get here?"

"A couple of hours ago, your mom let me in."

"Oh okay, are you good?"

"Yes, just needed to get out that house for a little bit. Why? You said I could come through anytime I wanted to!"

"Calm down, heffa, I did and I meant it!" she laughed.

"Now that I know you're good, let me tell you about

this guy I met on the bus today. He was fine as hell. Brown skin with beautiful green eyes and he had enough meat on his body. You know I don't care for those boney niggas. He had the sexiest white teeth and waves in his hair. Looking like he just stepped off the cover of a magazine. But even with all that, his ass was on the bus, and I do not date guys who ride the bus. What are we going to do, ride the bus to the movies? He asked for my number but I didn't give it to his carless ass...Next!"

Tamika rolled her eyes at Reka.

"How could you say something like that when you don't have a car your damn self? He could have been a doctor for all you know."

"Do you know any doctors that ride the bus?"

"No" Tamika replied, "but maybe it's because I don't know any doctors."

"True. But I'm sure if you did he wouldn't be riding the bus."

Reka laughed so hard she made Tamika start laughing. Tamika took the pie she made while she waited out of the oven.

"Girl, you are never going to change. You are going to be a wrinkled, old, and lonely with a little weenie dog named Weasel." Tamika said laughing.

"Bitch, look who's talking! You're baking pies for the fuck of it and no, I won't and if in some fucked up way I do, it will only be because my rich husband died."

"What the fuck? Your ass is crazy." Tamika said pulling the letter she wrote Maurice out of her purse." Read this before I go and your dinner is in the microwave. You can thank me later."

Reka read it.

"It's cool. Now seal the envelope and send it to the bitch."

Tamika hugged Reka.

"I love your crazy butt."

"I love you too now go mail that letter."

Tamika grabbed the keys, pie and letter, and headed out the door.

Six months later with no money coming in, Tamika went back to work. She was a nurse at Centennial Hospital where she met her husband. She was a little scared to return back not knowing what her coworkers would say about what happened with Maurice. To her surprise, no one asked her anything. She was sure they knew because he was fired for no call, no show and it was on the news and in the local newspaper. They made her feel just as welcome and comfortable as they did when she first started six years earlier.

Tired from her first day at work she fell out the couch. Her kids came in, saw her sleep and just put the mail next to her purse on the table. When she woke up, she saw a letter from Maurice sitting at the top of the pile. He had been sending them the entire six months he was in jail. She normally threw them away without opening them but she decided to read it.

"Humph," she said after reading it. "The same old lying fucker!"

Tamika ripped up the letter and threw it in the trash. She decided to put a stop to this a.s.a.p. She sat down at the table and wrote a response letter that read:

Maurice,

Please tell me how someone can give you their all. Love you when no one else did or would. Stay with you

after you betray them. Even when there was no more trust, I stayed with you and had your back. Yet you still treated me like shit! It's sad because you said you would rather suffer than be with me. Well, you are about to eat those words. Everything that I am and ever will be is riding on this one. I will no longer allow you to control my feelings day to day. God has been good to me, and He and my children are the only things that keep me going when I want to give up. So you can take your apologies and your bullshit lies and take them to hell with you. I said I wouldn't allow myself to love again but I will not give you that type of power over me. God has forgiven you for what you did and so have I. However, I will never forget. So with that being said, all your shit is at ya mama's house. You can see the kids whenever you want whenever you get out. And best of all, we will be divorced soon! So please don't call me, write me or think about me unless it has something to

do with the kids. I pray that you change and find someone worth changing for because obviously that woman wasn't me. Oh, I forget you did, my little sister! Deuces"

Tamika.

Two months later the letters from Maurice had stopped and secretly, it bothered Tamika that they had. She was mad at him and knew she'd never forgive him or her sister for their betrayal but there was something about him begging for another chance that made her feel wanted. Her first year of being without him was approaching and she was starting to feel alone. Yes, there were plenty of men flirting with her but none worth giving her time. She remembered her talk with Reka about passing the guy up because he was on the bus and decided to listen to her own words. She made her an account on one of those online dating sites and poured her heart into the profile she made.

She checked it daily for about a week but there still wasn't a man to give her the mental simulation that she needed. She needed more than sexting and it seemed like that was all the men had to offer her.

"Did this fool just say he liked my soup coolers?" Tamika thought to herself. She called Reka and said, "Has any ever told you have sexy soup coolers?"

Reka fell out laughing.

"Yes, dinosaur pussy. That means you have nice lips."

"Oh," Tamika said laughing. "That's what he should have said then. That's all I wanted to know." She hung up before Reka could say bye.

Still offended Tamika didn't accept his friend request. She went through another two boring conversations and then received a message that read:

"Look, I don't want to sound, or come off like a

cornball, but your picture is what attracted me to u...It was your eyes, and them juicy soup coolers lol. No offense, but they are sexy, I mean really sexy and you are too...now I'm rambling. You've probably heard everything I said to you a hundred times or more on here so how about I start over by saying, hi!

Tamika closed it out without responding. She went to his pictures to see what he looked like.

Damn, he fine. Light skin, bald head and confident. Maybe I should see what he's about.

Tamika went back to the message and accepted the friend request. Almost immediately, they began talking.

"So, what made you request me?"

"I was looking for my future wife and your picture showed up. I hope you don't think I'm a stalker or anything, lmao. I just thought you were pretty and said to myself why not compliment you. I will write you when the game goes off if you're still up."

"Okay that's fine."

One talk after the game turned into Jason and Tamika talking every day for hours at a time. Jason owned his own business and he had one son named James. He and Tamika had a lot in common. They had both been married and both of their marriages ended horribly, leaving them with trust issues. Jason told Tamika every day how beautiful she was and how much he liked conversing with her. Every day it seemed harder and harder for them to hang up the telephone with each other. Tamika, had problems sleeping at night and the doctor prescribed her sleeping pills but she hated taking them. Jason would not hang up the phone at night until he heard her swallow her meds. This made Tamika fall for him even harder. She thought it was funny how someone could care so much about her from so far away.

"Hey baby, how are you?" she damn near purred into the phone.

"Hey boo, what's up?"

"I think I'm falling for you way too hard and way too fast. I wonder where this is going. Maybe I should just fall back before I get hurt."

"I hear you. I'll fall back because I do think you're really pretty, cute, and sexy, but I don't want rush anything. I am sexually attracted to you, I'm sure of that! I can't stop looking at your pictures. I go on your profile to look at them every time the vision of you in my head fades away, but what does that mean? Is it love or lust?"

"I have been hurt in the past and I am praying that God gives me a man that is deserving of me and wants the same things in life that I want. And most of all, someone that loves me and that . I can trust. I think you are sexy too but I can't stop myself from wondering if I can find what I'm looking for in you."

"Thank you for the compliment. It's not every day I hear that. I'm glad that you accepted my request, and until we figure this thing out you definitely have a real friend in me! I hope that your prayers will be answered. I've been praying for a woman that will love, and accept me for me. A real woman who is willing to meet me halfway and understand I'm going to make mistakes. For someone who is truthful, compassionate, sensitive, and beautiful on the inside as well as the outside. You have to be specific in prayer for real!"

"So you're saying that I should be praying for another man? Because I just prayed for God to send me someone that will love me the same way I love I love them and I met you."

"No,I'm not saying you should pray for another man. I know u just want a companion, and a great friend, and someone who will love you and accept you for you. I'm only saying that I'm not perfect and it will take me some time to be everything you need but I'm willing to try to be him."

That was all Tamika need to hear to fall in love with her online boyfriend and no one around her understood it. Yes, they did talk on the telephone for hours and emailed each other throughout the day as she worked but Reka and everyone around her felt like Tamika needed more. In their eyes, she was playing married with her pen pal that she would never meet who probably was living a double life through the internet.

Reka had become fed up with the dream world her best friend was living and was ready to wake her up but she didn't have to. Jason made a call to Tamika and told her that he had to turn himself in to the police for a warrant. He told her he had a week to get things together before he turned himself in and he was unsure how long he was going to be incarcerated. A week passed without her hearing anything back from him and Reka became the pillow Tamika cried on. Day eleven of Jason's disappearance he finally called Tamika.

"Hey, baby. I'm in here. I just wanted to let you know. I'll talk to you when I can, okay?"

"Okay. Give me the address so I can write you. I've been calling Booking and Information every day and they kept saying that they didn't have anyone by that name in their system. I've been so worried about you baby."

"Yeah, I just turned myself in a few minutes ago and I don't want any mail. I don't want anything that reminds me of the outside, okay?"

"Okay," Tamika responded and the call ended. She

looked up at Reka who was standing over her hoping for some good news.

"Girl, he just turned himself in but something isn't right. How in the hell is he going to call me from his phone when they take it when you get booked? And what nigga you know in jail don't want any mail, don't know how long he's doing and ain't said shit about a court date or lawyer? I didn't say shit while we were on the phone but he must think I'm stupid, huh?"

Reka laughed.

"I don't know, girl."

"I'm not stupid," Tamika said as if she was trying to convince herself that she wasn't. "This muthafucka is probably shacked up with some bitch and don't want to tell me. I'm taking my ass home!"

Tamika got up, grabbed her suitcase and left with her

ass on her shoulders from the days she spent crying over something that wasn't real. She thought about all the men she passed up over the past four months to put her faith in her ghost man. Her pussy has been marinated as she waited for the day they would meet and it was all fake. She wasn't a fan of sleeping around but hell, she was a woman and she wouldn't deny her need to be touched or stroked in and out of by a man. The eighteen months of finger fucking herself was pissing her off more than it provided relief. Red Hot was becoming her nickname again. She vowed years ago to kill that part of her but these sorry ass men she continued to fall for kept the bitch in her alive. She was so deep in her thoughts of finding a man who could relieve her build up that she missed Jason's next call. She listened to the voice message.

"Hey baby, it's me. I just wanted to let you know I was okay. I will call you again when I can. My friend from church works here. He is CO, so he'll be letting me use my phone from time to time and his laptop when he can."

Okay. Maybe I'm tripping, Tamika thought.

As stupid as that sound, she still wanted to believe him and give him the benefit of the doubt. but deep down inside she knew it was a lie. Knowing she was playing the fool she began sending him poems and letters by email to cheer him up. She sent cards and continued to talk to whenever he could call. Things never seemed to pan out. When Tamika would ask him if he went to court and what happened. He never had a straight answer. Then, conversations between them went from all day, every day to once a day, to once a week. Tamika hadn't heard from Jason in three weeks so she decided to send him one last message and move on.

"Hey you, I'm sitting back patiently waiting for the day when I will see your smile and hold your hand, for you to tell me that you miss me and you're finally ready to see me face to face. If for some reason I don't get that chance to hear your voice again or ever see you face to face I will thank God for the short time that I had with you. Until I hear from you again I pray you have blessed days."

"Girl, my brother just went and got me a phone because my cousin works at sprint, so you know we got the hookup now. I'm not forgetting about your ass but this how jail life is."

"I'm glad you didn't and when are you coming home and don't say soon?"

"Soon, as soon I can. I still got one more court date. I know I said that was the last one but I still haven't gotten my time yet. Oh and when I get out I may be moving out of state as well."

"Out of state where?" Tamika asked surprised.

"Nevada, to start a new life with you...Sike! I'm

thinking we will move to Washington. I get out there and get us straight and then send for you and your kids or whatever."

"Washington and what's the move for?"

"It's time for new life. My business isn't what I thought it would be. I'm turning all the business over to my best friend."

"But, why Washington? Is there a reason or did you just picked a state."

"I have friends out there, and my business will get off a lot faster out there."

"Okay sounds like u have it all taken care of, that's good that u have a plan. So, when will all this be taking place?"

"Soon!"

"You really think your slick. You know exactly when

your ass going."

"I sure do."

"I know you do but the reason for not telling me? I tell you everything that's going on with me."

"Well, I just don't want to jinx myself."

"What, that's not jinxing yourself! So tell me this," Tamika asked hesitantly. "Where do I stand with you?"

"You stand up straight! I'm just kidding. I mean we cool as hell woman."

"Stop playing; you know exactly what I mean!"

"I mean really, I can't have a relationship with you if we're thousands of miles away. That would be weird and I love the fact that were so cool and that you're helping me out in my time of need. I think we will have a wonderful friendship for a lifetime. You're beautiful, sweet, crazy, sexy, cool, and wonderful to talk to. I think about you a lot."

Tamika was pissed and ready to give him a taste of Red Hot.

"Okay Motherfucka, that's what I needed to know. Basically, I have been waiting on you for nothing. It was nice knowing you!"

"Woman cut it out! It wasn't for nothing. And you know that. Tamika, since I've been locked up, I haven't made any money and I'm pretty much broke. I can't come into a relationship with you broke. You don't want a broke nigga. I have a lot on my plate, and it wouldn't be fair to you if I did that and you know this, so shut up!"

Tamika realized he was nothing but a liar and full of shit. As she read his words, the more enraged she became and the more she wanted to hurt him. The only way she knew how without being in his face was with words.

"Your ass was broke before you went to jail if that's where you really are, so don't use that as an excuse. That's some bullshit. Like I said, it was for nothing because I would not be waiting on you for a long distance friendship. What the fuck? I could go outside and make a friend. You know what the hurtful thing is? My best friend wanted to tell me I was stupid for even talking to you but she didn't because I was so gone over you. I'm sure she thought I was weird for thinking that when you got out of pretend jail, somehow things would work out between us. You're a broke ass joke to me and I should have picked up on the bullshit sooner. Always needing a few dollars wired to your personal account but lying and saying it was a business account. You pretended to be locked up so you wouldn't have to ask me for money anymore. You thought I'd just keep depositing it so your fake as CO friend who works there can withdrawal it and put it on your books. Keep lying about being locked up and watch how that shit happens. I hope that they put your lying ass in a cell with a nigga who eats ass. Bye bitch!"

"Wow. Tamika this really hurts. I really appreciated you and everything you did for me but since you feel like that it's cool. I hope all will be well with you since you think I'm a liar and have time to play games. I won't be broke for long! May God bless you for coming into my life and loving me in such a short time. I guess good things and good people come and go like the wind. Oh and by the way, tell your best friend who you're listening to, to KISS MY ASS!"

Tamika didn't hear anything from Jason until three months later when he sent pictures of his release document, his brother picking him up from the jail house and a one way ticket to Washington. When she tried to respond back, his account had been deactivated.

Crying, she decided to call Al an old friend that she

had a previous relationship. Whenever Tamika wanted to hear the truth about something, she would call him. Despite their breakup when they graduated from high school, they remained good friends. He told her,

"You have to stop giving all of you up too soon. That goes for love and anger. Red's hot, do you remember when everyone we use to kick it with would say that and how often you heard it? It wasn't good then and it sure in the hell ain't good now. You're knocking on 40 and going through the same shit you were facing at 16."

"I'm not trying to," she interrupted. "What can I do to make it stop? I just want to be in love with someone who's going to love me back!"

"I don't know, Red. What I will say is next time, make sure that his feelings are the same as yours before going all in but most importantly, if you haven't gotten right with God, nothing you touch will grow. God is the only man you need to focus on right now."

"Ok, I'll go to church and focus on him. Thanks!"

Trying to keep the promise, she made to herself by joining a church, spent every available moment she had helping the church and organizing group outings for the church's youth. She prayed constantly for God to send her a man that would be God-fearing and love her and her children as his own. She made a promise to herself not get mad and hurt over a man again and the only way to do that was to stay single. Mingling wasn't even an option. She wrote a letter to her sister and now ex-husband, Maurice letting them know that she forgave them.

One day, while visiting a Christian bookstore, Tamika ran into a friend she used to work with as a teenager at the ice cream parlor.

"Excuse me." He said recognizing her without completely seeing her face.

Tamika turned around. Standing in front of her was a tall, brown-skinned man with golden brown eyes smiling at her.

"Yes," Tamika answered.

"Is your name Tamika?" The man asked.

Yes, it is. Do I know you?"

"It's me, Robert from the ice cream parlor when we were a lot younger." He laughed

"What, look at you. How have you been?"

"I've been as good as you look."

"Thank you," Tamika said, modestly. "Did you just get out of jail?" she asked instantly remembering that she heard he had been sentenced to fifteen years or better the last time she inquired about him.

"No, those days are long gone. After I graduated

school, I made a promise to myself to man up and make the most out of my life. All I do is work and go to church. I hang out with the guys every now and then, but that's about it."

"Are you married?"

"Yes, but my wife's an alcoholic, so if you were to ask her you might not hear the same answer. Guess you can say I'm dealing with a lot right now."

"I'm sorry to hear that."

"Are you?" He responded, with a smile.

"I'm divorced and I do have two kids. Why don't you take my number down and give me a call sometime so we can catch up."

"Okay, cool."

Tamika and Robert exchanged numbers and left the store. About a month after seeing Robert, Tamika was at

Albertson's grocery shopping and ran into him again.

"You never did call me," Tamika said, smiling.

"I didn't know if you had a man and I didn't want to cause you any unnecessary drama." "That's funny because that's the same reason I hadn't called yet. I didn't want your wife to trip out on you."

"She knows all about you. I told her that I ran into you just in case you did call. Some of our classmates are hooking up later. If you want to go, let me know."

"I have a meeting at the church tonight. I can't. I'm sorry."

"How about I go to your church meeting with you?"

"If you want, you're welcome to come," Tamika answered.

"It's a church; everyone's welcome." Robert laughed.

Over the next three months Robert and Tamika saw a lot of each other. She would counsel him about alcoholism and her daughter Raven, would babysit his son Robby, from time to time. She started having feelings for Robert but never acted on them because of his situation. She hadn't met his wife and didn't want to do anything to put their marriage in jeopardy.

*****

Robert, just home from work, opened the door to find the house in a complete disaster. He looked around for his wife and son. Deana was asleep in the bed and Robby was in his bed soaking wet and crying. He took him out of bed, bathed him, made him a bottle and put him to sleep. He walked over clothes that were over the hallway floor just to handle the tasks. When he was done, he went downstairs to see if Deana had at least made dinner. Dishes were everywhere. An empty bottle of gin was on the counter next to a half full small bottle of the same poison. Trash was spilling over in the trashcan to the floor like a waterfall of debris. He shook his head in agony and started to clean up. His phone rang. It was Tamika.

"Hey, babe, let me call you back."

"What's wrong? You don't sound too good."

He told her about the house, Deana, and the baby.

"Get the baby, get in the car, and come over here."

Without debate, he grabbed Robby and drove to Tamika's house. Tamika opened the door and took Robby from him.

"I have some food cooked on the stove. If you want to take a shower, there are clean towels in the hallway closet."

"Thank you, T. I appreciate it. I'll take a quick shower."

"If you look in my closet, there's a box of clothes that goes to the church. You're welcome to whatever you can fit," Tamika yelled through the bathroom door. "Me and Robby are going to the store."

She grabbed Robert's keys from the table and drove to his house. Tamika sat Robby, still sleeping in his car seat on the couch and went up to the bedroom to see if Deana was awake. Tamika tried calling her name and shaking her to wake her up. She wouldn't budge she closed the bedroom door and picked up all the dirty clothes from the floor. She found an empty basket to put them in and sat them in the closet. She washed the dishes and swept the floors. When she was done, she and Robby got back in the car and headed back to her house. She saw Robert sleeping on the couch. She looked at the clock and realized she'd been gone for two hours. She kissed him on the forehead and he jumped up. He thanked her for dinner and the shower and went home.

Robert walked into the house to find it spotless. He went upstairs, and opened the bedroom door to checked on Deana who was still sleeping. He sat on the bed trying to figure out who cleaned the house. Maybe, Deana's mom came by, he thought but after calling her she said she hadn't been there. Tired, with only a couple of hours before he had to be at work, he put Robby to bed then opened his drawer to grab a pair of sleep shorts and there was a handwritten note:

Smile,

I just wanted to make you happy. You deserve to be!

Tamika.

Robert smiled and went to bed.

He woke up thinking about the note he found in the drawer. He couldn't believe that Tamika would do something like that. Just the thought of it made her even sexier than he already thought she was. He called her but her phone went straight to voice mail.

"Tamika, I just wanted to thank you for everything that you did for me and Robby last night. If there's anything I can do to repay you, please let me know. Give me a call when you can."

Tamika listened to the message, but stalled on calling him back. She hoped he wouldn't start asking her questions about how she felt because she wasn't ready to answer. The note was a mistake but she was wrapped up in her feelings after seeing his wife passed out drunk that she wrote her truth. Not wanting to cause him any confusion she decided not to call him back.

Two years had gone by when Tamika decided she would go see her sister Alicia. Alicia just looked at her. Tears fell from her eyes.

"Do you know what I'm going through in here?" Alicia asked.

"Do you know what I'm going through out here?" Tamika replied.

"Look, Tamika. I'm sorry for what I did. I didn't mean to hurt you. I love you. I really do."

"I really don't want to talk about it."

"How's Mom?"

"She's fine. She adopted a baby last year. I don't know why she would do something so stupid. I tried to talk her out of it, but she did it anyways. A bad ass three year old little girl but she's the prettiest little thing I've ever seen."

Alicia started to cry.

"Why are you crying?"

"I have to tell you something," Alicia said.

"What?"

"The reason mom insisted was because the baby is mine."

"What are you talking about; you done fucked a guard up in here?"

"No, it's Maurice's."

Tamika's first thought was to break the glass and choke the shit out of her. But she didn't.

"Does he know?"

"I'm not sure. I wrote him, but I don't know if he got it. He never responded back."

It took everything in her not to break down in front of Alicia.

"You know they gave me 10 years?"

"Yeah, I know. Now you have 10 years to think about

how you will spend the rest of your life making it up to me. I have to go. I love you, Lee-Lee. After everything you've done to me, I still love you!" Tamika got up and left.

Tamika waited for the bus to come around and get her. A part of her wanted to tell the police what she did and go on with her life. The other part of her wanted her sister to sit and rot for what she did. When the jail bus pulled up, she got on. To her surprise, there was Robert.

"I didn't know you worked here."

"I don't, you would have known where I worked if you would have returned any of my calls. It's been three weeks. Why are you avoiding me?"

"I'm not. I've just been busy."

"Too busy to call me back? I filed for a divorce."

"When did you do that?"

"The Monday after I left your house. I had time to

think about my life, where it was, where I wanted it to be and who I wanted it to be with."

"Wow, that's a big move. How did Deana feel about it?"

"She didn't like it, but it's my life. I have temporary custody of Robby. I moved out the house and into a two-bedroom apartment."

It's time for me to get off."

"I miss you," Robert yelled, as she walked of the bus."

She turned around and smiled.

Tamika walked into the house to see Raven playing with Robby.

"When did he get here?"

"Robert dropped him off on his way to work earlier."

"Why didn't anyone tell me?"

"You were at the prison."

"So what time is he picking him up?"

"I'm not sure. I think 11 or 12."

Tamika picked up Robby.

"Hey, baby, you miss me?"

Robby looked at her and smiled. She kissed him on the cheek and put him down.

"Make sure you feed him and keep him dry."

"I know, Mama."

The doorbell rang at a quarter to 12. Robby was asleep in the bed with Raven. Tamika threw her robe on and opened the door.

"Well, damn, you're sexy even when you're trying not to be."

"Hush and get in here; it's cold."

Robert came in and closed the door.

"Robby is sleeping. If you want, you can leave him here and I will drop him off to you in the morning."

Thanks; that's cool. Do you want to take a ride with me?"

"At this time of the night?" Tamika asked, curiously.

"I need to vent a little."

"Let me put on some clothes."

"You can go like that if you want. We aren't getting out."

"No, wait, while I get dressed."

Tamika slipped on a dress she had next to the bed. She threw on some sandals, grabbed a coat and they left. They must have driven for hours with Robert telling her all that happened over the three weeks she hadn't seen him.

"I'm getting sleepy; let's head back to my house."

"Okay, that's cool. But I have a question."

"What?" Tamika asked.

"What do you think of me?"

Tamika gave him a blank stare.

"What do you think of when you think of me?"

He grabbed her hand while waiting for her to answer.

She looked into his eyes and said, "I think you're a man of honor, wisdom, and love. A man of honesty and hopefully, a freak. When I think of you, I think of all the men out there that are about to be jealous of you and all the women out there that wish they had the guts to be me right now."

"Why do you say that?"

"Pull the car over."

"Why?" he asked.

"Just pull it over."

He pulled over as she asked. She reached over and unzipped his pants. He leaned his seat back.

"No. We're not staying in the car."

"Sit on the hood of the car."

"But the headlights are on."

"I know. I want to see the look on your face when you cum."

He sat on the car and she started sucked lusciously on his warm penis. She was on her knees and all he could see was her face threw the light. He pulled her hair, which was usually a sign that he was about to cum. She stood up as if she knew

"Get back in the driver seat."

Curious, he did. She slid the seat back and said, "No, not yet. I think I want to ride this one out."

Robert still didn't know where Tamika was going with this.

"Lay the seat all the way back. Now drop the top."

Panty-less, she sat in his lap, making sure to sit her hot pussy on top of him. She put her hands on the steering wheel and started the car. She put the car in drive and drove off fulfilling her fantasy of fucking her man on the freeway in the driver seat of a convertible while driving.

When they were done, Tamika pulled the car over. She got off of Robert and walked around to the passenger side. She got in, leaned forward, and kissed him.

"Now what was that question again?" Tamika teased. Robert was speechless.

"Let me get you home."

"Naw, I think I want to see your new spot."

Robert was in shock. His place was just fine. He was ready to return the favor 10 times over. They pulled up to his apartment. He grabbed her hand and led her to the door. He unlocked the door, picked her up, and carried her to his bed. He gently kissed every inch of her body. Tamika wondered if she was making a mistake. She didn't want to go through the last two years all over again. The kids loved Robert and Robby and so did she.

"Robert, stop."

"What's wrong?"

"I'm scared."

"Scared of what? I won't hurt you."

"I know you won't physically, but you might emotionally."

Robert came up from between her thighs and lay next

to her. He pulled her close, wrapped his arms around her, and they fell asleep.

Tamika woke up to her phone ringing.

"Ma, where are you? Your car is here."

"I came with Robert to his house to get clothes for Robby."

"You could have said something, dang," Raven said, laughing.

"I'll see you in a bit; bye, Raven."

Robert looked at her and said, "Sit down." Tamika sat on the couch.

"Look, I'm not going to do anything to you that you wouldn't want me to. You took me by surprise last night and I just wanted to make you feel as good as you made me feel."

"That's good, but I don't want to be hurt."

"Tamika, you have known me since middle school. You knew I wanted you back then. I think everything that happens for a reason. God brought you back into my life for a reason. My son loves you and so do I."

"You love me?" Tamika asked.

"Yes, I do. Why do you think I filed for divorce? I'm not the type to play games and before I asked you to marry me, I wanted to be sure that I had a clean slate before making you my wife. I know you heard about my arrest and sentence, but I was wrongly accused. And after serving two years for something I didn't do, the evidence that I was innocent surfaced. I vowed to give it all to God and the men like me, that are locked up for nothing."

Tears streamed from her eyes.

He wants to marry me? She thought.

Tamika was quiet the entire ride home. When they pulled up to the house, Robert faced her.

"Look at me, T; do you love me?"

"Yes."

"Will you marry me?"

"Yes."

"Raven and David, come here please." Tamika yelled while walking into the house. Raven came out the room holding Robby.

"David isn't here," Raven said, coming down the hall.

"Where is he?"

"Tracy's house, why, what's going on?" Raven asked, curiously.

"I guess I better tell you," Robert said, smiling. "Will it be okay if I married your mother?"

Raven sat down.

"No!" She yelled, before running to her room and slamming the door.

Robert and Tamika looked at each other and then Tamika ran to Raven's room. When she opened the door Raven yelled, "SIKE!" then fell out in laughter.

Looking at Robby, she said, "So, I guess you're going to be my little brother."

Robert grabbed Robby, kissed Raven and Tamika bye and left.

"Reka, girl, I am engaged!"

"Whoa! I didn't know you were seeing anyone."

"I didn't either. I guess actions speak louder than words."

"Well, to whom?"

"Robert."

"Robert who? The guy that you went to school with you?"

"Yes."

"Damn, I haven't even met him yet. So when can I meet him?"

"We are going to plan an engagement party and everyone can meet him then."

"I thought he was married."

"He's going through a divorce."

"Oh, that's too bad, but I'm happy for you. So what colors are we using? What's the date? And ooh, girl, I need my hair done. I better get in the gym; you know it be fine ass men at weddings." Tamika laughed.

"Girl, you are something else. I'll talk to you soon."

Tamika was excited about the wedding, but she still hadn't confronted her mother about Brianna, Alicia and Maurice's daughter. She drove to her mom's house. When Brianna saw her coming to door, she ran to it. It was hard for Tamika not to love her. Brianna took to her almost immediately. Tamika grabbed her and gave her a kiss.

"Hi Auntie."

Brianna tried to say it, but it sounded more like, "bye nunny". She was neglected by the first foster parents to take her home from the hospital's jail ward. Her speech classes were working but for almost four years old, she still talked as if she were one. Tamika's mother looked at her.

"I am so sorry that I didn't tell you, that was the reason why I took her in. Yes, your sister told me you visited her and forgave her."

Tamika didn't say anything. She put Brianna down and hugged her mother.

"Mom, I would have done the same thing if I were in your shoes."

Her mother smiled.

"So what brings you here?"

"I'm getting married."

"To who?"

"Remember Robert that went to middle school with me, the boy that was always in trouble?"

"Yes. Oh, Lord, please tell me you're not having a jail house wedding?"

"No. He hasn't been into any real trouble since tenth grade. That other stuff we heard about, he was found innocent. Look, I just stopped by to tell you. I have to get back to work. We are having an engagement party. I'll call you with the details when I get them."

Tamika rushed back to work.

Months had passed and Robert's love for Tamika grew more each day. Now that his divorce was final, it was time for them to celebrate their love with an engagement party. While Tamika ran through the house cleaning everything she came a across, Raven set the mail on the table Tamika was wiping off and waited for her brother to do the talking.

David said, "There's a letter from Dad in there." He didn't want her to read it so he snatched it out the pile and threw it on the ground.

"That's okay, baby. I want to read it."

Tamika gave her son a warm smile and opened the letter.

Dear Tamika,

I know I'm the last person you want to hear from. I thought I should let you know that I received your

letter. I'm sorry I hurt you. Alicia wrote me and told me that she was pregnant a few years back. She said it was mine and not knowing if that's true or not has bothered me every day since I received it. I don't know if she had the baby and I don't know if it's mine but I don't want to keep anymore secrets from you. I hope that you find someone that will treat you the way you deserve unlike I did. Please tell the kids I love them and I'm sorry for not being the father that they needed, I still love you.

Sincerely,

Maurice.

A tear fell from her eye. She dried it and went on cleaning and cooking for their engagement party. Robert walked in and hugged her behind.

"Are you okay?"

"Yes, babe, I'm good. Guess it's the onions I was

chopping up."

"That's why I didn't want you cooking. I'll pay to have it catered."

"Babe, we can't afford that," Tamika said, walking back into the kitchen.

"There's something I haven't told you."

"Not again?"

"No, it's not anything bad but if you're saying what we can't afford it then I need to tell you money isn't an issue for us."

She laughed.

"Money is an issue for everybody. Just because we both have jobs doesn't mean we can go blowing money. We have three kids."

"And our three kids will be well taken care of because

of that wrongful incarceration case. Tamika, I'm a millionaire."

"You're a what?" Tamika laughed so hard she started crying.

"I'm serious. I lost a lot of time sitting behind bars and the government couldn't give me none of it back so instead they gave me 2.7 million dollars and a typed up apology letter."

Tamika, still laughing, said, "You've been living in an apartment with no furniture for over six months. I'm sure they gave you something but nothing about you say millionaire, Robert."

"I own those apartments and Robby and I needed to move quickly so I moved into one of those. I'm left her that house and now that we have a big family we need something bigger. No offense, but this shithole you had with your ex, I'm not comfortable living in that's why I haven't moved in. We are only staying here until our house is finished."

"Finished? What; it's being built?"

Tamika could feel the honesty in his words and almost passed out.

"Baby, are you okay?"

"Yes but why didn't you tell me about this, why didn't you tell me you were rich?" Tamika asked.

"I needed to know that the next woman married would love me for me and not my money. Deanna knew from day one and all she ever did was spend it. But I would much rather spend it spoiling someone who deserves to be spoiled."

"Wait. You don't expect me to quit my job and sit around the house like she did do you?"

"No, that's completely up to you."

Tamika sat down.

"Is this still a secret or is it okay if others knew?" She had to ask because the urge to run her mouth to Reka consumed her.

"It's completely up to you, babe. I'm going upstairs to get dressed before your family and friends arrive."

"What about your family and friends?"

"Well, that's another thing you should know. When you get accused of breaking into someone's home and raping their 14 year old daughter, your family and friends disappear. Even my mama assumed I was guilty and told me I was dead to her. It didn't matter what I had to say, my past of being a bad ass won the fight. When I got out and got my money I paid off her house and had the bank send her the deed with a letter from attached explaining what had transpired. I haven't reached out because I'm comfortable being a ghost and everybody else can kiss my ass." He planted a kiss on her lips and went upstairs before Tamika could tell him that he needed to work things out with his mother like she had with her sister.

Reka was the first to get to Tamika's house that evening.

"What's with all the catered food?" Reka asked. "Girl, you making money like that?"

"No, Robert did it."

"Damn, this shit is expensive. This isn't a cheese and crackers party, this is a steak and lobster shindig." she laughed.

"Don't start," Tamika said with a giggle. "You can sit wherever you want. Robert will be down in a minute. I'm going to go throw my dress on."

Reka couldn't believe how nicely the house was decorated. Robert walked in the back door as she peaked inside her best friends cabinets to see what else she had new. He came up beside Reka and said, "Hey, pretty lady."

She turned to look at him.

"Look what at the shit the cat has drugged in, did you catch the bus here?" She laughed.

"No, I drove this time."

She looked passed him to the convertible parked on the side of the house. She couldn't tell the make of it but it screamed expensive.

"That's good, you still want my number?"

Robert laughed at how stupid and shallow Reka sounded.

"No, I have a lady now."

Rolling her eyes, Reka replied, "I guess, new car, new lady, huh? How do you know my girl Tamika or are you one of Robert's friends?"

Before he could answer, Tamika walked in.

"I see you two have met."

"Yes, we have," Robert answered.

"Robert, this Reka, Reka this is Robert."

Reka was shocked.

"Oh, wow. This is the guy I told you about that I saw on the bus." Tamika gave her a blank stare. "Remember, I told you there was a guy that asked for my number and I said no because he was on the bus."

"Oh, yes." Tamika laughed then continued with, "I told you would pass up a good thing being shallow." Reka rolled her eyes and smacked her lips.

After the party, Reka pulled Tamika to the side.

"You know I think it's pretty fucked up how you tried

to clown me in front of your man."

"What are you talking about, Reka?"

"Calling me shallow and saying that you told me I would pass up a good thing like it's cool you're talking to a nigga I used to talk to. You could have kept that shit to yourself."

"I don't have time for this shit. Either you're happy for me or you're not. You could have been me right now, but you were so shallow that you passed up a good guy because he was riding the bus. Furthermore, how the hell was I supposed to know he was the same guy? That was two years ago. And if you want to get technical about the shit, I knew him years before your ass rode the bus, so either shut the fuck up with this bullshit or get out."

"Now you're putting me out over a nigga? Fuck you, T!" Reka yelled. "You think you're the shit now because your man a got money. I bet he ain't sharing shit with you though. He still got you and the kids living in Maurice shit!"

"Like I said, get the fuck out my house."

"Bitch!" Reka yelled, as she walked out the door.

"Dang mama, why she acting like that?" Raven asked.

"She has issues. She had one too many glasses of wine tonight and acting jealous. She'll calm down when she sobers up."

Reka left Tamika's house and went straight to the police department to tell them that Tamika set up Alicia and Maurice. She was drunk and pissed but it was jealousy that sent her through the doors. Her drunken state was obvious so the officer who came out to take her statement told her they would look into it. She didn't like how he kept asking her how many glasses of wine she had as if he wasn't taking her serious so she went home and wrote

Maurice a letter.

Hey Maurice,

I am writing you tell you that although what you did to Tamika was fucked up, what's even more fucked up is how she lied to the police and set you guys up. She told me exactly what she said to get you that attempted murder charge and I have informed the police but I don't think they believe me. You should contact your lawyers to see what they can do on your behalf. I know that's my best friend but she's dead wrong and I'm willing to testify if I have to. She's getting married soon to a millionaire. You will need to hurry up before he moves her out the country and she gets away with doing you wrong!

Love and miss you,

Reka.

Reka waited until she was sober and debated on sending the letter that would put her best friend behind bars. She wanted to see how important their friendship was to Tamika and waited for her to call but that call never came.

A few months had passed since Tamika and Reka fell out. Tamika felt bad that Reka hadn't picked up the phone to apologize for trying to rain on her parade, so she called Reka to apologize for putting her out instead.

"There's something I have to tell you before you decide you want to apologize."

"What?" Tamika asked.

"Well, remember when I told you that I told Robert that I didn't date guys that rode the bus."

"Yes."

"Well, before all that, I kind of gave him head on the

bus."

"You did what?"

"He was fine! I didn't tell you because you would call me a hoe and I've never done anything like that before. It was a secret I planned to take to the grave."

"Just tell me everything now." Tamika said.

"Okay, the bus was really crowded and the only seat open was next to me. He sat down and we flirted back and forth for a little. I was feeling kind of horny and he was fine, so I laid my head on his lap and I felt his dick get hard. I put my head under his jacket, pretended I was sleep, and gave him head while he played with my pussy."

Tamika hung up in Reka's face. Reka called her right back.

"Look, just hear me out. I should be apologizing to you. And I am sorry. I asked him not to say anything to you because he wanted to tell you so don't get mad at him. You guys deserve each other and besides, like I told him, I don't date dudes on the bus. I just got a little jealous because he had money after all. And like you said, I fucked it up by being shallow. It was like a, I told you so but yet, you had him. I love you like a sister. Please forgive me."

The entire story was a lie but she wanted Tamika to feel like she had the upper hand. She wanted to Tamika to have a fear of them every day she spent married to him. Jealousy had won.

"I'm not even going to trip; all that was before me. He loves me today and I'm marrying him. I will be over there so you can get on your job and help me with this wedding. We have six months to get it all done."

"I'm happy for you; I know things will work out. I can't wait to help make this day special for you both!"

*****

Robert stopped by the newsstand on the way home to pick up the local paper. An old friend of his was killed in a car crash and he wanted to read his obituary since going to the funeral where everyone thought of him as a guilty man wasn't an option. When he got the paper, he was shocked to see Maurice in the paper. Maurice was one of the many men he wanted to help prove his innocence's but he wouldn't let him. Maurice was still in love with his accuser and wouldn't dare reopen the case if it meant she'd go to jail in his place. He decided to do his time and take it as karma for his actions.

Robert knew Maurice's story well but read the article to get a different view of the incident. As he read his eyes almost popped out of their socks as there was new evidence found to prove that Maurice and is crime partner Alicia were innocent and that his ex-wife had indeed cut herself. The name Alicia sound familiar but what put the puzzle pieces together for him was reading Tamika named as the ex-wife. Robert hadn't known anything about what happened. All he knew about Tamika's ex-husband was that they were divorced, his name was Maurice and that they divorced because he cheated.

Robert was furious and purchased all 10 papers the stand had left. He went home and clipped the article out of each paper. Two weeks later, when Maurice was released, Robert met him at the jail. He explained to him how he was supposed to marry Tamika and how he wasn't aware of anything that happened. He had a bond with Maurice and they shared a tear or two when they talked about their wrongful arrest. He felt like he betrayed a good friend by going after his wife even if it was unknowingly.

Robert took the articles he saved and placed them under the glass of Tamika's dining table. He cooked dinner for himself and Tamika. Robby, Raven and David were with Tamika's mom for the weekend as planned. He set the table and poured two glasses of wine. They talked over their meal like they always did.

"I can't wait to be Mrs. Robert Gunner!"

"I can't wait either. No secrets, I need to know before we get married, right babe?"

"No secrets. I promise."

"Okay, good."

He stood up from the table and kissed her on the forehead.

"Do you mind clearing the table while I shower?"

"Sure, babe."

Robert wondered how long it would take her to realize the papers were under the glass. Tamika cleared the table first then she sprayed Windex on the table and began wiping it. While she wiped, she noticed the clippings.

Robert was smart. He hadn't put any of the pictures from the article up. Tamika took one of the papers from underneath the table, sat down and read it.

"Maurice Ryan and Alicia Stokes will be released from prison as soon as the new evidence is verified. Although, we do have a witness, Ms. Reka Jenkins who is willing to testify that the victim did indeed lie about the night in question, until we can prove they are innocent, we will not arrest the victim, Tamika Strokes-Ryan."

Tamika dropped the paper and ran to her room. When she opened the bedroom door, Alicia and Maurice were standing there. Robert came out the bedroom.

"I think you were looking for me," Robert said.

Tamika stood there, in shock.

"How, when, you…" She managed to say but the words just didn't seem to come out right.

"Is there something you're trying to say? I think you owe all of us an explanation." Maurice said staring into her eyes with hurt and angry in his own.

"I don't owe you two shit!" Tamika yelled. "Robert, please, I can explain."

"Explain what, Tamika?" Maurice said, "How you set us up, how you cut your own wrist, or how you're a lying bitch chasing down my boy for his money? I told you there was a guy trying to help me get out for three years and what you had to do and you never responded. You sent two fucked up letters instead. So what did you do, research his money?"

"I never opened your letters!" she screamed and then faced her sister. "Alicia, please," Tamika cried. Alicia just looked at her with her own eyes full of tears. All she could say was,

"I know fucking your husband was wrong but putting

us in jail for attempted murder, that's fucked up. I've been away from my daughter too long, I can't stand the sight of you."

Tamika, crying, ran out the room. She grabbed her purse from the kitchen counter and ran out the door. Just as she opened her car door, two police officers approached her as news vans pulled up and Reka jumped out the passenger side of one them.

"Tamika Ryan?"

"Yes?"

"You have the right to remain silent."

The End

Glass Candy

Keyshon loved to sit in his window and watch people as they came and went. He made a game of guessing their occupations and marital status by what cars they drove. Every now and then two legs instead of the usual four wheels would spark a new game. A game that ended with his hand covered in his favorite lubricated lotion.

Suzy loved walking to the store. It was the only time she got to enjoy fresh air and the only exercise regimen she could stay faithful to. On her walk she would see Keyshon in the window staring at her and from time to time she'd give him wave. When she first moved into the neighborhood she thought it was weird that the man three houses down sat in the window the entire day, staring at the outside world like a kid on punishment but after learning from the lady she rented her house from that he had lost his finance in a car accident due to a drunk driver and that he found solace behind the glass, she began growing a soft spot for him.

One night Keyshon walked to the store to grab a beer and his favorite peanut butter M&M's as he occasionally done. The only thing different about the trip was it was snowing outdoors, and he wasn't wearing a coat nor clothing that would shield him from the weather. When he got home his fingertips had turned blue which was contrast to the red tip of his now running nose. He turned the thermostat up, took his usual seat in front of the window and enjoyed his bring home take as he defrosted. It was late, so he wasn't expecting to see much but that wouldn't stop him from admiring how beautiful his street looked with the new fallen snow.

Suzy could see him turn up his beer can from her living room window and the roles turned. It was her turn to stare at him as he had done her, but her look came with a list of questions. She wondered if he had attempted to date after losing his almost wife and if having a girlfriend or wife was no longer a desire of his? She hadn't seen anyone going in or out his house but him. He was handsome but dark, mysterious but as open as he kept his curtains and that's what made Keyshon her type of man. Not having anyone herself, she decided to find out if she had a chance to help bandage his open wound.

Suzy put on her red lace panties and bra, slipped on her high heel boots to match, touched up her hair, put on her trench coat and walked out the door. She spotted a car parked just in front Keyshon's window. Slightly nervous she walked to the car sat on the hood. She waved to Keyshon and he waved back as usual, thinking nothing of it. Slowly, Suzy started to undo her jacket button by button. She was shaking because it was cold but that wasn't the only reason. She'd never done anything like this before and if it didn't work in her favor, she'd more than likely so, pack up and move away to dodge his future looks.

Keyshon didn't understand why this beautiful woman he often daydreamed about pleasuring was sitting on the hood of a car as it snowed but he was interested in watching to see what she would do next. After opening her jacket to give him a look at her lace she stood up in front of the car and blew him a kiss. She motioned for him to come to her but shocked by what was taking place he didn't move. Which was fine with her as she grabbed her breasts and kissed each one gently.

Once she realized he wasn't going to walk away she laid on the hood of the car freezing from head to toe, but she was so wrapped up into what she was doing that she kept going and her lack of fear kept her warm. She continued to rub on her breasts as she ran her hand down her stomach and into her panties. Keyshon's dick was hard as a rock and he stood up to get a closer look. Suzy moaned as she slipped her fingers in and pleasured herself. He couldn't hear it but the thick cloud of smoke coming out of her mouth in the cold made the audio necessary.

Keyshon was completely turned on decided to join in. He unzipped his pants grabbed his dick and pleasured himself while watching her do the same. He was so into stroking his meat that he threw his head back against the chair, closed his eyes and enjoyed it. When he was done he opened his eye and didn't see Suzy. He opened the curtains wider, but she wasn't there. Curious of her location he opened the door to go out and look for her. Suzy, with her coat open was standing there waiting for him.

"Are you looking for me?" she said smiling.

He responded with a kiss. Kissing her deeply he picked her up and carried her to his bed, a bed he hadn't slept in for months. It was too painful to sleep in it alone and the coach made him feel like he was laying comfortably in his lover's arms.

Releasing her lips from his he began planting soft kisses along her collarbone, but Suzy wasn't feeling it. Making love had never made any of her things to do list. All she wanted from her neighbor was a nice long fuck, with ass slapping, hair pulling and name calling. She wanted him to take all his months of loneliness out in between her legs and that's exactly what he did. After wrapping her hair around his wrist to use it as the bungee cord that bought her wet pussy back to his raging hard dick, Keyshon nutted up her back and left his final drips upon her neck. He handed her a shirt to put on.

"Thank you for a wonderful evening, "she said to Keyshon as if the night was spent at an expensive restaurant followed by ballroom dancing.

"No thank you for the erotic show you gave. It beats staring at snow any day. When will I get to enjoy it and you again?"

"I don't know but I'd advise you to keep sitting in your

window staring out at the snow. You never know what you'll see or get if you don't look!"

The End

THE PENSTRESS

Mr. Peanut Brittle

Finding out Roman cheated was one thing, but not having a clue of who the bitch he'd been dipping in and out of was something else. The handwriting on the envelope wasn't familiar and the words used weren't enough to allow Shayla to use her imagination to draw a picture of slut. As much as Shayla tried to get over it, she wouldn't get closure until she actually saw her.

Why Roman, why?! Did she look better than I did; was she fat, skinny, with long hair, or short hair? What made you want her so much more than you wanted me? These dumb ass visions I keep having of you and some other woman play out in my mind and I can't get them to stop. How am I supposed to cum on the dick I no longer feel like is mine? Even the way you touch me was

new. The way you held me, you've never held me like that before. Is that how you cuddled with her? If you sexed her like this, no wonder she doesn't care that you're married.

You better thank God that the urge to throw up had over powered the urge to slap the shit out of you. I am trying my best to deal with it the best way I know how but you expect me to let it go like the shit didn't happen. You expect me to put your dick in my mouth like there isn't another bitch's fragrance in the hairs covering your nuts.

Do I let the last sixteen years of my life go or do I step up my game and make it work? All I know is, when I catch the bitch it's on and not because of the affair. You fucking her was foul but her knowing about me and not caring made it worse. She knew you were married and didn't give a damn. The disrespect is what I won't tolerate. She has me wondering if I should even

let you come back home if she's still willing to fuck you knowing about me. Should we go to counseling? What should I do with you?

Shayla closed her diary and placed it in one of her old purses she hadn't used in years. Going to work was something she just wasn't in the mood for. However, she had to. Shayla clocked in at 2pm. She tried hard to keep a smile on her face but there wasn't shit for her to be smiling about. It was Monday, the most hated work day of the week, and they were busy. If her bladder wouldn't have felt like it was about to burst she would have accidentally worked through her designated lunch break.

During her lunch, some of her coworkers asked her what was wrong. Shayla didn't know them well enough to put her business out there so she fed them a quick lie about being slightly under the weather. There was someone person she could talk to that she trusted, Trish. Trish was her supervisor and someone she hung out with outside of work. They had been friends for the length of her three years working at the crisis line for teens.

"Girl what's wrong?" Trish asked. "How are you on the phone helping other people when you can't help yourself? And don't lie because the pain is written all over your face."

"I can handle it," Shayla said with a fake smile.

"That's the same thing our clients said to themselves right before calling us. I guess I'll just wait for your anonymous call through the switchboard."

"Shayla, can I talk to you for a min?" Anthony asked stepping into the break room.

"Sure."

Shayla stood up and gave Trish a smile in defeat as Anthony, another floor supervisor followed her into her office.

"What's up?" Shayla asked.

"I have a couple of school referrals that Andrew can't take. Would you mind taking them?" He begged more than asked.

"I would but I'm already way over what I can handle right now, is there anyone else that can do it?" Shayla was busy but it was her mood making her decline.

"No, I tried everyone else before coming to you." Anthony placed the folder on her desk and whispered in her ear thank you. "And whatever is wrong with you, I'm sure I can fix if you let me."

"Thank you," Shayla said laughing as he walked out the door.

Anthony was tall, dark skin with a slight caramel tint, rough around the edges but still handsome, and a self-proclaimed cocksman who chased after the next best nut he could get. Something about him reminded her of a smooth piece of Peanut Brittle. He was the talk of the office and all the women wanted him. Anthony was a flirt and he was known to have many women. Nobody in their right mind would leave one cheater to creep with the next.

After work, Shayla went to Trish's house to talk. The last place she wanted to be was home.

"So what's going on Shay?" Trish asked.

"Girl, Roman walked in the house without his ring on Saturday night and when I asked him where it was, he said 'in the car', like that was normal."

"And your responds was?" Trish asked handing her beer.

"I asked why wasn't it on his finger and he said it was getting too tight so he took it off for a while but he'd go get it in a minute."

"I hope you didn't believe that lying bastard," Trish laughed.

"I can't lie, I wanted to believe him that's why I went to the car to get it and what I found was an envelope that had his ring inside of it with a note that read, "baby you left this on the nightstand; wouldn't want to get you into any trouble", written on the outside of it.

"Bitch stop playing!" Trish yelled.

"Shit, I'm not playing; I went inside, threw it at him, and he pretended not to see it. Then, after an hour of him playing dumb I couldn't take it anymore. I slapped his ass and started throwing his shit out the door."

"He didn't say anything at all?" Trish asked.

"Nope nothing. He sat there feeding his face as if it was nothing. I wanted to stuff the biscuit he was eating so far down his damn throat he'd feel it in his ass."

Trish laughed so hard she started crying. The situation wasn't funny but the way Shayla delivered it was. The faces she made and the way she said it felt like a stand-up comedy act.

"Then his stubby ass friend comes walking down the street."

"Wait," Trish said laughing. "Not the one that walks

like this?" Trish began to walk like Randy, Roman's friend, by stretching one leg out in front of the other in a slow motion.

"Yep, his sloppy, fat, no neck having ass but the look I gave him made his ass turn right around and walk the other way."

"So what did Roman do when you slapped him?"

"He stood there looking stupid like always. That's how I know he was up to some shit. He took the slap like he deserved it and didn't say shit about it."

"Did he at least get his clothes out the yard?"

"Yeah, after his dumb ass saw me driving over them."

"Shay you are crazy."

"No I'm not, that was me showing him that I was brokenhearted but crazy was up next. I made sure to let the tire roll into the oil that had leaked in the driveway that I asked his ass to clean up a hundred times. Then I ran back and forth over the shit until he started dodging the car to pick it up."

"Damn Shay, please remind me to never to piss you off," Trish laughed.

"He's lucky I didn't burn it along with the envelope and ring. Bitch, Angela Bassett in Waiting to Exhale by Terry McMillian is my icon!" she said finally laughing at her own words.

"So how did you find out he slept with her or was the words on the card enough?"

"The words were enough but he told me. He had the nerve to say that the problem isn't me, it was him and he needs help. He kept saying that I didn't do anything wrong."

"Why do they love to use that lame ass lines?" Trish added.

"Right, because I know damn well the problem ain't me. It's him, ALL him!"

Trish fell out laughing again.

"When you're mad you're funny as hell. So what do you want to do because I can throw my sweats on and we can go kick his ass," Trish said laughing. "You know I have zero tolerance for this type of bullshit."

"I really don't know what to do Trish. I cried all night, I'm tired of crying."

"I know you are, Mamas." Trish said consoling her.

"Do I forgive him or let this bitch have what I worked for, for the last sixteen years?"

"Only you can make that decision, Shay. If I tell you what to do and it doesn't work in the end, you will be mad at me."

"No I won't Trish, and you know that."

"That's what your mouth says but you are the one that has to put up with his shit or the way you're going to feel without his shit. Either way, I'll leave that one for you to decide on but what did the neighbors say with their nosey asses?"

"They weren't home."

"Good, you already have a lot on your plate and don't need them peeking around. I will be here if you need me."

"I do need you, that's why I'm here."

"What do you need me to do?" Trish said with her hands on her hips.

"Well, I figure since he cheated on me why not just cheat back on him."

"What?"

"You heard me Trish."

"What the hell will that fix and out of curiosity who would you cheat with?"

"Anthony."

"Who?!" Trish asked shocked. "Why, Anthony?"

"Because he's fine as hell and I can tell he knows how to slang that dick, look at how he talks around the office."

"But you know how he is and he's slagging that big ole dick to everybody." Trish responded trying not to let the laugh escape her lips. She hadn't fucked Anthony but she did grab her a handful of him a few times when he came flirting.

"So, that's a good thing. I'm not trying to fall in love. Just casual sex when I want it and how I want it."

Trish released the laugh.

"I am going to tell him," Shayla said and then thought about it for a minute. "No, I changed my mind."

"Naw, too late," Trish said still laughing, "I'm telling him!"

Shayla made it home in time to cook dinner and get the kids to sleep. The sight of Roman made her stomach turn. *What was he doing here anyway?* She thought, *He should have been at his brother's house.*

"Why are you here Roman?"

"Because I live here."

"Why don't you go stay with the bitch you been fucking?"

"You are the bitch I've been fucking."

"Okay. Well go stay with the bitch that had your ring. You know the place well enough, being you left it on the nightstand."

"What the hell are you talking about?"

"Don't try to act stupid now, I'm sure you read the envelope just like I did," Shayla screamed at him. "And what kind of whore are you fuckin' with anyways?" Trish continued. "She obviously knows you are married and doesn't care. I am so over it. Please just get the fuck out."

"I'm not going anywhere Shayla."

"Okay fine. Don't go."

Shayla slammed the bedroom door in his face and called Trish.

"You are the closest thing I have to a sister and if I call my brothers they will be over here kicking his ass."

"It's cool girl. You have to be at work early tomorrow so get you some sleep."

"I know and I'll try."

"Alright, I'll see you tomorrow."

Shayla hung the phone and started crying. *I don't understand what I did to make him do this to me.* She kept asking herself this repeatedly until she fell asleep.

The next morning after clocking in Shayla ran into Anthony in the hallway.

"So what's up Shayla?"

"Nothing what's up with you?"

"You know what's up with me? Anthony said smiling. "I hear you want me."

"What?" Shayla said smiling, "I didn't tell you that."

"You didn't have to. Your eyes say it all. Plus, a little birdie told me for you."

Shayla walked away mumbling, "I'm going to kill Trish when I find her."

She walked around the office until she spotted Trish. She snuck up behind her and covered her eyes with one hand and wrapped the other hand around Trish's neck in a mock strangulation.

"I know it's you Shayla." Trish said laughing already knowing why Shayla had her in the hold.

"You know I'm going to kill you, right?" Shayla said.

"I guess you have to kill me because he already told me to invite you over so he can come kick it." Trish freed herself from the hold and walked away smiling.

Shayla spent the rest of the day trying to avoid Anthony as best she could but it seemed everywhere she turned he was there. All the ducking and dodging she had done didn't matter because Trish talked Shayla into coming over her house after work for an off the clock meet and greet with Anthony. When Shayla got there, Trish's boyfriend Brian was there and not too long after Anthony pulled up.

Shayla was excited and nervous at the same time. She did have a huge crush on Anthony but she hadn't flirted with another man in sixteen years.

"So where's my hug?" Anthony said to Shayla once he was settled in.

She stood up and hugged him. It felt so good to be hugged. That was something she didn't feel often because her husband wasn't affectionate.

"Trish do you need help with the food?" Shayla asked.

"No I got it."

Anthony grabbed Shayla's hand, "let's go talk outside on the porch."

"Okay" she responded following him out the door.

However, there wasn't much talking. She told him what was going on with her. He hugged and kissed her. He told her everything would work itself out. He gave Shayla a big long hug and a kiss on the forehead. He sat in the chair on the porch and Shayla knelt down in front of him her heart racing. Anthony took her head into his hands. At that moment she knew it was about to go down. Moreover, there was nothing she could do or wanted to do to stop it. Anthony looked her in her eyes and she stared back. That was the first time she noticed how beautiful his eyes were. *Fuck it,* she thought as she unbuttoned his pants, pulled his zipper down and reached in to feel his penis that had been warmed as it was entrapped in his boxer briefs. Anthony took her hand and rubbed it along his dick. She watched it rise wondering if she should stop touching it. Instead, she pulled it out and kissed the tip of it. She ran her tongue along the shaft and looked up to see Anthony laid his head back on the chair. She looked toward the window and then at the door to see if anyone was looking. Knowing that they were alone Shayla took him into her mouth. The faster she bobbed her head the wetter her mouth got. She was throwing her neck like she had never done with her husband and allowed his chunky dick head to rub against her tonsils. Surprisingly, it didn't take him long to cum, but even more surprisingly, she found herself upset that she couldn't suck on him longer. His nut was sweet like the Peanut Brittle nickname she secretly gave him. He then stood up somewhat feeling defeated by her throat and bent Shayla over the chair to redeem himself. Slowly, entered her from behind as he fought the sensitivity in his dick and with every stroke, the tingling lessened as she moaned. He hushed by covering her mouth with his hand not wanting anyone to hear them fucking outside like it was an hourly ho motel. When her wetness splashed against his thighs like a fat bitch jumping into a shallow pool, he grabbed her hair making sure she could feel him pulsating inside her. Shayla clinched her muscles as he released himself in her pussy like he was the true owner of it. Feeling untouchable Anthony, zipped his pants back like it was his routine to get some pussy on the porch and Shayla ran into the house heading towards the bathroom as the reality set in and that she had just been fucked.

Trish was still in the kitchen and Brian was making

drinks when Shayla came out of the bathroom. Trish looked up just as Shayla tried to hurriedly pass by her to go back outside.

"You had to clean yourself up huh?" Trish said laughing.

"No," Shayla said with a smile of shame, "I had to pee." she closed the door and went outside. Anthony was leaning against the wall.

"I'm sorry, Shayla. I know you didn't picture your first time on a porch."

Shayla looked at him confused.

"Well I mean your first time cheating. I know this dick is so much better than what you're getting at home but I should have given it to you in a better place."

Shayla just smiled. Actually, it was perfect to her. It was different and she always wondered what it felt like to have sex out in the open.

"No it's cool" she replied with a smile. "I never

pictured myself cheating so there were no expectations but that's cocky of you to think it's better than what I'm already getting."

"Cocky yes, but it's the truth. I could tell how you came on my dick he hasn't been hitting it right." he concluded with a chuckle.

"Is that why you didn't you use any protection?"

"I should be asking you is that why you let me nut in you without a rubber on. I went raw in you because I wanted you to feel all of me and I know you're clean."

"No you don't."

"Yes I do."

"How do you know I'm clean?" she asked curiously.

"Are you trying to tell me you're not? If so, I can run to my car and grab my gun instead of waiting until the doctor gives me the fucked up news." he said raising an eyebrow.

"No crazy, I'm clean but what made you assume that I

was?"

"Shit, because I'm assuming your husband is the only person you're fucking."

He was right about that. Shayla hadn't been with any one besides her husband. The thought never crossed her mind to cheat until he did it. She was only asking Anthony the questions because she wanted to know if he was fucking everything he could raw.

"Well, you still don't know that as a fact. I could have sexed someone before I came here and that wetness you felt could have been his nut."

"Girl if you don't knock it off, before I have to knock you off." Anthony said laughing.

"So, are saying that you just go around sleeping with women without protection because you think they are clean?"

"No just you." he replied.

He stood behind her and hugged her until Trish called

them in to eat. Shayla couldn't wait to get home to call Trish. However, on the way home all she could think about was how stupid she was for not using protection. Thoughts of STDs and an unwanted pregnancy filled her mind. She thought that cheating would make her feel better but it didn't. She pulled into her driveway and stood at the front door. She heard voices so she knew Roman had company. She slipped into the house and into the bathroom. She bathed and hopped into bed. She fell asleep wondering what work would be like the next day.

Shayla woke up to slamming doors and cursing. She hopped out of bed.

"What's going on Roman? Why the hell are you slamming doors?"

"Alice called with some bullshit about money." *Oh Lord, here we go,* Shayla thought to herself. "Every time I look around, she's asking for money for this and money for that." Shayla looked at him and closed her door back.

Shayla had nothing to say about his relationship with his daughter. She was 19 now and was always asking for money like she wasn't legally grown. Alice never completed anything she started, this included school. She got pregnant at 17 and continued to run the streets so now her mother, Ava, is raising her son. She started stripping at some club and is now the talk of the town as whispers spread that she can be paid to do more than to take her clothes off. At this point in their marriage Shayla, could care less about what was going on with him and his daughter. All she wanted to think about was Anthony. She wondered how he would treat her at work, and the shit Trish was about to lay on her once she found out that they fucked on her porch.

"Shayla, Shayla?" Trish yelled at her.

"What!" Shayla responded snapping out her thoughts of the night before.

"Well damn, I've been calling your name for hours

now."

"Stop lying; I haven't even been here an hour," Shayla laughed.

"So what happened last night?"

"Nothing."

"Stop lying, Shay. You were all smiles; so I know something happened."

Shayla looked up. "Nothing."

"I already know because me and Brian looked through the window. We saw your ass out there brightening up the dark sky."

Embarrassed Shay told Trish all about it and all Trish could do was laugh. She waited a few hours before coming clean to Shayla.

"I was lying. We didn't look through the window. I just knew yo' nasty ass was outside doing something."

Just then Anthony walked by. He stopped and winked at Shayla, hugged Trish and kept going. Trish sat at her desk with a smile on her face.

"Look, don't get your heart all into it because you know how he is. He got bitches and he ain't no good. That's my boy and I love him but it's true. So just, be careful. Have fun but keep your feelings in check."

"I will, you know I'm not looking for a replacement. Just a little fun every now and then."

Shayla, craving McDonald's rushed to the elevator at lunch. She felt someone standing behind her so she turned around. There was Anthony. She tried her best not to smile. The elevator opened and they got in. They rode in silence to the breakroom. She grabbed her purse from her locker and sat it on the table to look for her keys. The room was empty and she saw Anthony standing over her out the corner of her eye. She looked up at him.

"What?" she said.

He smiled because with her sitting down, him standing in front of her left her starring right at his penis. He leaned in closer. She backed her chair up. He leaned forward again. She backed up again.

"Why are you playing, I have to go?"

"I'm not playing, and besides there's no one in here."

"So what does that mean?" Shayla asked with attitude.

"It means that it will only take a minute for you to give me some of that good ass head you gave me last night."

Shayla laughed, "Nope gotta go."

Anthony wouldn't move so Shayla unzipped his pants pulled out his penis and licked the head of it. When he reached down to hold it up to her mouth she slid her chair back and ran to the elevator.

"Awe, that's fucked up; you just gon' leave me standing here like this?"

"Yep!" Shayla said laughing as the elevator door opened and closed with her in it.

Shayla laughed all the way to the car. She spent the rest of her workday catching up on old cases she had that required a follow-up. Although she took calls from the crisis line she was a social worker by degree and most of her cases consisted of teens who were being abused. She was fortunate enough not to have to do any fieldwork thanks to her cases being established from the incoming calls. Nevertheless, overall, Shayla loved her caseload and she loved the kids she helped to keep living.

Going home for Shayla meant having to deal with issues she wasn't ready to deal with. Roman's cheating hurt her in many ways and she hated to admit it but she was in need of a crisis line to call for the brokenhearted. She started to question everything she did and had done. The way she dressed. The way she cooked. The way she talked. Walking into the house Shayla saw Roman passed out on the couch and his phone ringing off the hook. Normally she wouldn't answer his phone but since it was going off continuously, she decided to pick it up.

"Hello?"

"Hello?" said the other woman's voice on the phone.

"Who would you like to speak to?"

"Roman; isn't this his phone?"

"Yes it is and who are you so I can see if he wants to take your call?"

"Who are you?" the voice replied.

Shayla could see where the call was going so she speed the bullshit up.

"First of all who the hell are you to be asking me who I am, and second of all it might be his phone but I pay this bill."

"Well since you're into paying a nigga's bills, how about you pay his child support he hasn't been paying."

"I should have known it was your ass, you really need to get it together Ava. Alice is grown and he doesn't have to pay you child support because you decided to move y'all grandson in!"

"Who is Ava? My name is Patrice."

"Excuse me?" Shayla said confused "Patrice who?"

"No trick the question is, who are you and why you asking me who I am?"

"I'm his wife, BITCH!"

Click.

Shayla looked at the phone. She put it back to her ear but the call was over. She threw the phone at Roman and it hit him in the head.

"Get your ass up! Who the hell is Patrice?"

Roman looked up holding the top of his head.

"Patrice who?"

"Your baby mama Patrice, that's who."

"What?" "That must be Ava playin' games with you again."

"You know what; I am so tired of your ass get up and go stay with your momma."

Roman sat up and Shayla stood in the doorway with it wide open. The neighbors started to come out and peep out of windows. Shayla was always so quiet and reserved but this time she wanted to make a scene to let him know she was serious. She fussed and cussed until someone called the police and when they arrived Shayla had them escort Roman and the rest of his shit out the house. The police told her they couldn't keep him from the home without her filing a restraining order but she knew he wouldn't come back, not after seeing how mad she was. When they left she apologized to everyone that was still outside and went back in the house to call Trish.

Trish grabbed her ringing phone from her purse.

"Hey Shay what's going on?"

"I just had that fool escorted from the house."

"Why, he didn't hit you did he?"

"No, another one of his bitches called and had the nerve to tell me to start paying child support for her baby." She slightly twisted the story but that was the way she heard it.

"Wait he has another baby?"

"Apparently."

"Wow, so now what are you going to do?"

"I'm going to tell Anthony to come over."

"Why don't you come and kick it over here until you calm down instead?"

"Ok, I'll be there shortly."

Shayla cleaned up showered and headed out the door to Trish's. She pulled up in the driveway and before she could open the door to get out the car there was Anthony pulling in behind her.

"What's up Shay?" Anthony said sounding sexier than ever.

"What's up with you?"

"Trish told me to come through. Are you straight?"

"Yeah, I'm good."

Shayla walked toward the door with Anthony following behind her.

"I have food and drinks. You guys know where everything is. Shay‚ let me talk to you for a second, please." Trish led Shayla into the bedroom. "You know if you need to stay here tonight you're welcome to."

"I'm good girl. That nigga ain't crazy, besides I could always take Anthony big peanut brittle ass home with me."

"Yeah, okay, then you will really need the police."

Shayla made herself a drink and sat next to Anthony.

"Why are you so quiet?" he asked.

"No reason."

"I have a couple of movies y'all can watch or you can turn on some music," Trish said, handing the DVD case to Anthony.

"Either or, it doesn't matter to me" Shayla responded.

"Music it is" Anthony said.

"Shay can you answer my cell for me please" Trish asked showing off her wet hands from washing the dishes.

"Hey Brian, how are you?"

"I'd be doing better if your girl would hurry up and come get me?"

Trish turned to look at Shayla realizing that she'd forgotten to pick Brian up at the sound of his name.

"Tell him I'm sorry and I'm walking out the door now." She grabbed her purse with her wet hands and hurried out the door.

Anthony looked at Shayla.

"So, what you wanna do?"

"Nothing, listen to some music."

Anthony didn't care for her answer. He stood up and pulled Shayla off the couch. With more force than she thought was necessary he turned her around and Shayla held onto the couch.

"What are you doing?" she asked while looking over her shoulder at him smiling.

"You'll see" he said snatching her pants down. He spit in his hand, rubbed his fluid on his meat and the rest around her opening before entering her. After a few pleasurable strokes Shayla said, "Anthony stop; Trish is going to be pissed ,that's my girl and I'm not trying to disrespect her house."

"Now you know damn well why she left us here, besides she won't know anyway."

Shayla tried to move but he was stronger than she was and the dick was good, she gave in. With each sway of her hips he moaned and slapped her ass which forced her to sway it the opposite way. Before she knew, it was over. Shayla was a little pissed because it was over before it started but she didn't say anything. That was twice he got off quickly but at least the first time he was able to get it right back up. This time, he looked as if he needed a nap so she laid in his arms until they both fell asleep.

Trish walked in the house and yelled, "Get y'all asses up."

Shayla opened her eyes and closed them back.

Anthony said, "We wouldn't be sleep if you hadn't left us here for hours."

Trish laughed. "You know how it is. One stop became many."

Shayla stood up, yawned and stretched. "I have to go, it's late."

"I'll walk you down. I'm leaving too. Trish, come lock up baby, we're leaving." Anthony said.

After work, the next day Shayla had Roman meet her at Denny's so they could talk. Roman came in smelling good with a new haircut and wearing new clothes. He sat at the booth, told his brother, who he had been on the phone with, that he'd call him back and looked at his menu.

"So, what's up? What do you want to talk about?"

"You're cheating and what you plan to do now." she snapped.

"It's not you it's me, I already told you that. I am overwhelmed and feeling smothered. Marriage is starting to feel like jail instead of love."

"And you couldn't just say that instead of cheating?"

"I tried to tell you?"

"How did you try to tell me?"

"I left hints here and there."

"Hinting at shit and telling me shit is two different things."

"Look, it is what it is. I tried to tell you." Roman whispered and Shayla almost spit her food out when he said it.

"This bitch really has you feeling yourself because you've never talked to me like that before."

"I'm just being me. I can't change what I've done all I can do is move on." he finished his sentence with a nonchalant shrug.

"Thank you for such an insightful meal. Guess, I'll start looking up divorce lawyers."

Shayla wiped her mouth, threw her napkin on her plate

and walked out. She drove home knowing that she made the right decision to sleep with Anthony but payback was a greedy bitch and she wasn't done, especially after hearing what he had to say about it.

Roman came in about fifteen minutes after Shayla and slammed the receipt down on the table.

"What's that?" Shayla asked.

"Your receipt."

"No, you mean your receipt; and since when do I have to start paying for our meals?"

"Since you decided to put me and out."

"Hmmm. Now that could be a problem being your ass is still my husband. In fact, I've decided to go ahead and forget about all the bitches you've cheated with and work on me so I can be better for you."

"And when did you make this decision?"

Truthfully, she hadn't thought of the words until they came out of her mouth but she answered like she had.

"I thought about it on the ride and I need to change some things about me. I know I haven't been very attentive lately and I've stopped making you a priority in my life, and baby all that changes today." Roman looked at her as if she was crazy. "But there's one thing you have to do for me."

"What?" Roman said with a puzzled look on his face.

"I want to know every name and details of the other relationships you're in or had. I want to know if you've ever gotten them pregnant, if you paid bills and who has kids by you. I need to know the whole nine yards if you want to try to make it work. Do you want to try to give us another chance?" her anger sent tears down her cheeks.

"Yeah I do but you know you don't really want the answers to those questions."

"That's what I need in order to move on and I need to know where I went wrong."

Roman put his head down feeling fucked up inside

knowing that none of his cheating was by the fault of Shayla.

"And I'm going to need that by tomorrow. You can write it down or you can tell me face to face, it's your choice."

To her surprise, Roman blurted out, "Okay baby."

Shayla cleaned up the house, ran Roman a bubble bath and massaged him down afterward. He was feeling so good that he went straight to sleep. Shayla rubbed her hand along his penis, but he didn't budge. To her surprise kissing him on the neck didn't wake him. She knew if she was going to make a move she had to do it now. She grabbed his cell phone, a piece of paper and wrote down every number in it. She put the phone back, slipped into her nightie and went to bed. The next morning Shayla woke up to Roman kissing her down her back. Every touch from him made her want to throw up but the thoughts of her next move overpowered those thoughts. She turned around and kissed him. Shayla forced a smile to appear, "Good morning babe, it's such a nice day for a new beginning."

Roman kissed her neck.

"Sure is."

He took her hand and ran it up and down his dick. *Damn it can't get any worse than this* Shayla thought. She reached into her nightstand and pulled out a condom.

"What's that for?"

"My protection."

"What type of protection, and from whom?"

"Your other bitches. But if you don't want to use it, it's okay. I have to get up for work anyways."

Roman took the condom and put it on. Shayla turned away from him and backed her ass into him. The last thing she wanted to see was his face. Roman slid his head under the covers and kissed her thighs. Shayla didn't move. He grabbed her thighs and attempted to open them but Shayla didn't budge. He came up from under the covers.

"What's wrong?"

"Nothing, we don't have time for that, I'll be late for work."

Shayla rolled over, lifted her legs onto Roman's shoulders and pulled him closer to her. She sucked on his nipples and kissed on his neck. Not two minutes after he entered her he came.

"I'm sorry baby; it shouldn't be so damn good."

Shayla smiled.

"It's okay that was a bomb two minutes, daddy."

Shayla was happy as hell to have his tired ass off her. Glad that it was over, she went to the restroom, got dressed for work and left.

Before she could pull out of her driveway, she got a call from Anthony.

"What's up Anthony?"

"You sure are in a good mood" he responded.

"Only when I hear from you" she replied, backing out

the driveway and parking down the street.

"Cut it out," he laughed jokingly. "My mom needs to use my car. Would you mind picking me up and giving me a ride to work?"

"So you don't mind me knowing where you live?"

"No. Why would I?"

"From what I hear it's one of your rules not to let any of your females know where you stay."

"Exactly, none of my females, you're my friend."

"Oh okay so that puts me in another class?"

"Yeah you could say that."

"Hmmm. Okay text me the address and I'm on my way?"

Anthony was standing outside waiting when Shayla pulled up.

"Thank you." he said planting a kiss on her cheek.

"It's cool. You're only ten minutes away. Just don't make the shit a habit."

Anthony laughed, "Why not, you scared?"

"Scared of what?"

"Of what might happen."

"No, because I know nothing's going to happen."

"Okay, that's what you're mouth says Shay."

"No, it's also what my body says."

Anthony ran his hand up under Shayla's skirt.

"Stop, she said moving his hand away."

"Why?" he asked turning to look at her.

"Because I said so that's why." She said pulling into the parking lot. "We got here way too early."

"That's okay I have the keys."

"Good, I can get started on my work now and get a longer lunch. You're treating today since I drove, right?"

"Yeah, I'll treat. Treat you to some good dick."

"Uh, isn't this considered sexual harassment?"

"Only if you're complaining, and I haven't received any from you so far."

Hell no I'm not the shit is good, you just nut too quick Mr. Brittle. Shayla thought.

"Oh, I'm still feeling you out. I might voice one soon."

"Quit lying, but what about a ride home?" he asked.

"I can give you that and that's all you're getting." He winked at her and walked out.

"I didn't hear from you yesterday," Trish said standing in the doorway. "What's up with that?"

"I'm sorry; I was busy putting my plan into action."

"And by plan you mean?"

"Payback is a bitch."

"Be careful Shay, it's easier to just leave."

"I will Trish, why are you here so early?"

"I'm behind and need to play catch-up. You want to help me?"

"You know I got you. By the way, guess who rode to work with me?"

"Anthony did."

"Damn how you know?"

"I know everything, like how y'all fucked in my house and had it smelling like pussy soup." Trish said laughing.

"Bye. Get out my office now."

*****

"Shayla, do you want to leave early?" Anthony texted 30 minutes before their lunch.

"Sure do"

"Okay I'll be ready in an hour. Keep working until I come get you" Anthony was turned on by Shayla's rejection and talk of sexual harassment. It made him want to fuck her on his desk. He knew she wanted it just as bad as he did. He'd tried all morning to get some work done but getting Shayla back to his place was all he could think about. The way Shayla tried to ignore him on the ride home turned him on even more.

"Pull over Shay."

"Why?"

"Just pull over please."

Shayla pulled over and he reached over her to put her seat back.

"What the hell," Shayla blurted out.

"Just lay it back."

"Why?" Shayla asked.

"Because I want to get to know you better."

"What do you want to know?"

"How are things with your husband?"

"As good as they are going to be," Shayla answered.

"Why is that?"

"I'm done with him. I have my reasons for why he's still in my home. Others don't understand but it's not for them to because they aren't in my situation. What I really want to do is move the fuck away from here and start my life all over with someone who wants something better."

"Damn, you just gon' leave me like that and we just getting started?"

"I don't want to but if it's what I have to do then, yes."

"Well since you feel like that let me give you a reason to want to stay. Go ahead and take us to my house."

When they were inside of his house he urged her to make herself comfortable by removing her shoes. Shayla took her heels off and sat them next to the couch.

"Is there anything else you want me to take off?"

"No, not at the moment." he said taking a seat next to her on the couch. He grabbed her legs, sat it across his lap and started massaging her feet.

"That feels good." she moaned.

"It should I was a massage therapist before this job."

"Is that right?" Shayla took his hand and led it up her thigh. He started massaging it instead of replying. "Damn, what else you can do with those hands. It's getting hot in here."

"You want me to turn on the air?"

"No, I want you to turn me on and out."

Anthony unbuttoned her blouse, unsnapped her bra then carried her to his bed. He laid her down and massaged her entire body, with a soft kiss here and there. He turned her over and pulled her closer to the edge of the bed and laid his head between her legs. Gently he began sucking on her clitoris while using his hands to massage her breasts. Shayla grabbed his head in her hands and closed her eyes. He sucked and licked and when he stuck his two fingers in, her legs started to shake uncontrollably he could feel her muscles tightening as her sweet juices ran along his hand. He laid her legs back down and got up.

"I'll be right back."

Anthony went into the bathroom and brushed his teeth. After a shower, he ran a warm bath for her a bathed her slowly. She dressed when he was done and kissed him goodbye.

Shayla pulled up to the house with a smile on her face in shock that Anthony didn't try to fuck her this time. That smile almost disappeared as Roman met her at the door.

"Where you been Shay?"

"Trish and I went to eat after work."

"Guess you don't want the dinner I cooked you then?"

"I can take it for lunch tomorrow."

"Whatever." Roman said with an attitude.

Shayla was hungry. She and Anthony hadn't even stopped to grab anything to eat.

"On second thought I will eat. The food we had wasn't too good and we ended up throwing most of it away. I'm still hungry."

Roman warmed up the plate of food and placed it on the table. He sat down at the table across from her.

"So what have you been doing all day?" Shayla asked.

"Nothing, really. I took my grand baby to the park for an hour."

"She let you take the baby?"

"Yeah, she took Alice to orientation for school and

needed a babysitter."

"At least she's trying to do something positive, again."

"And then I came home and wrote this."

He handed Shayla an envelope with her name on it. She opened it to find the names she asked for the day before.

Lena Skye, messed with her for three months never pregnant. Asia Lee, messed with her for six months, was pregnant but had an abortion. Patrice Brown, messed with for two years, possible son, and is saying she's pregnant now. Tina Morgan, messed with off and on for five months, never pregnant.

Shayla put her plate in the sink and went to the bathroom. She took the list of names and numbers from Roman's phone and compared it to the list he'd given her. She placed a star next to each name on her list. But two next to Patrice's. With a smile on her face she put her paper back in her purse.

"Time to put this plan into action," she mumbled as she walked out the bathroom. She stood in the kitchen until Roman noticed her. "Baby this is what I think of these bitches." She tore the paper into pieces. "Our marriage means more to me than that."

Shayla grabbed and kissed him like she hadn't in years then walked into her room closed the door and laughed. She spent the next couple of days gathering all the information she could on the four girls. Lena was the easiest. Her address and phone number were found online. She also had a Facebook page that listed most of what she did throughout the day and where. She was twenty-eight, light skinned brown eyes and wavy long hair. She was a size ten as she listed on her page. She loved the beach and long walks in the park, outdoor dinners and had no children. Her profile listed her as single. After reading a few comments from her page Shayla realized Lena was into women as well as men. Shayla made a fake Facebook page with fake pictures and requested to add Lena as a friend.

Shayla then searched for Patrice Brown. To her surprise she was also a friend of Lena's. And so was Tina and Asia. *What the hell is going on here*, Shayla thought. *Damn I should have asked Roman where he met these females*. Patrice's comments referred to her having a Instagram page. Shayla decided to search her up. It came as no surprise to see her pictures were damn near naked. What did surprise her was that Roman had a page. *Now we're getting to the nitty gritty,* she thought. Shayla hurried to make her a page with fake pictures and decided that she would get to know Roman the way the other women had. She sent him a message and he replied right away.

Him: Damn sexy, the things I'd do to you.

Her: Hmm is that how you always approach a beautiful woman?

Him: Not usually but I couldn't help myself.

Her: Well if you can learn to speak to me

respectfully then maybe we can work some shit out.

Him: Damn baby, you're kind of feisty aren't you?

Her: Only when there's a need to be.

Him: So where's your man, baby girl?

Her: I don't have one, where's your girl or wife?

Him: I don't have one.

Shayla turned red to the face at him denying her. If she could have punched him in the face right then, she would have.

Him: So what's up with you giving me your number?

Her: I just moved here from Atlanta and I don't have a phone. This is my only means of communication for now.

Him: We are going to have to do something about that. Do you go out often?

Her: No I don't really know anyone here and I wouldn't dare go alone.

Him: Well, now you have someone to go with.

Her: Okay sounds like a plan to me, so why don't you have a girl?

Him: Y'all are a handful.

Her: Only if you're doing things you shouldn't be.

Him: LOL, maybe that's what it is. Why don't you have a man?

Her: Because I sometimes enjoy the company of a woman and most men can't handle that.

Him: That's too bad for them. I can handle that and much more. You should come check out this club I've been going to lately. I guarantee they will have a little something for you even if it isn't me.

Her: I will hold you to that.

Patrice sent a message,

Who are you, do I know you?

Shayla responded back immediately.

No but you can get to know me.

Patrice: And I would want to do that because?

Shayla: Because I heard that you would be a great friend.

Patrice: And you heard that from?

Shayla: From Roman, who I'm talking to him now.

Patrice: How do you know him?

Shayla: I met him through Lena.

I hope I'm not getting these names mixed up, Shayla thought.

Patrice: Oh okay. You know my girl.

Shayla: Do you mean girl as in friend or as in mate?

Patrice: As in, friend with occasional benefits.

Shayla: Wow, I like how you said that. I just moved here from Atlanta and I'm looking for work and friends to chill with in the meantime.

Patrice: Okay cool. Did Roman invite you down to the club?"

Shayla: Yes, he did.

Patrice: You should come down and kick it. So what's your flavor, men or women?

Shayla: A little bit of both. Men are too controlling and women are too emotional. When I find one with the right combination of both I'll settle down. Until then my nose is wide open to fun.

Shayla tried her best to sound convincing. She didn't know how she planned on pulling this one off. She would definitely need help with this one.

Patrice: Sounds like you and I will get along good.

Roman: It sure is taking you a long time to answer me."

Shayla: I'm sorry Roman, sweetie I have more than one conversation going on.

Roman: I thought I was important."

Shayla: No; sorry but that's something you have to earn.

Roman: Come down to the spot tonight. I will give you all the info before we end this conversation.

Shayla: I'll think about it.

Shayla saw Trish walking by and flagged her over.

"Can you do me a huge favor," Shayla asked.

"There you go trying to look all sad, what is it?"

"Do you want to go to a club with me and pretend to be some girl that just moved here from Atlanta?"

"Girl the shit you try to get me into," Trish said shaking her head no.

"Please?" Shayla begged. "Roman is trying to get with this bitch, and he denied me. He's never seen you before so you could easily pull it off."

"What's the name of the spot?"

"It's called Club Swing."

"Girl, do you know what they do in there?" Trish asked concerned.

"No, what they do?"

"It's a swingers' club. I'm not going, I don't want to be in the middle of this!" Trish yelled.

Shayla sat at her desk staring at the computer screen. She was angry and didn't know what she was getting herself into. *I can't be mad at Trish, it's not her problem its mine*, she thought.

"Okay well at least sit out front with me and spy with me," Shayla begged.

"Now that I can do" Trisha replied excitedly.

Shayla thanked Trish with a smile and responded to Patrice's message.

Thanks for the info, I will be there.

She immediately got messages from Asia and Tina saying,

Welcome to the club.

"What the hell is that supposed to mean?" Shayla said looking up at Trish.

Before Trish could respond, another message came in

from Patrice.

I just wanted to let you know that I won't be at the club for the next couple of months.

Shayla: Why not?

Patrice: I'm pregnant and Roman won't let me.

Shayla: Why, who is he your brother?

Patrice: No, he's the father of my son and the baby I'm pregnant with now. We aren't together, we just fuck on occasion; it's no big deal.

Shayla: Damn y'all be doin' the most.

Patrice: Not really, he's just a man to use until the real thing comes along. We all have been with him with the understanding that none of us will end up in a relationship with him. We don't want any issues with his wife.

Shayla: He told me, he wasn't not married.

Patrice: Girl he's married. She doesn't know anything about his club though.

Shayla: He owns the club?

Patrice: Girl yes, that club is his baby. I've never seen or met her personally but from what I hear she's a bitch.

"Who are you calling a bitch?" Shayla snapped. She was becoming more irritated by her husband's foolishness with every second that passed. She wanted to curse Patrice out but she wanted to find out the truth.

Patrice: I received my information about him being married from his oldest daughter's mother, he used to be a pimp and she was his bottom.

Shayla's heart dropped at the news. There was a lot about her husband she didn't know. She wasn't completely blind to his past because seeing how his daughter turned out confirmed that the apple didn't fall far from the tree. She always hoped her gut feelings about him and his ex were wrong.

Patrice: I can't wait to meet you. Why don't you

just come over here tonight and I'll tell Lena to come through so you can get to know her too.

Shayla: Okay just send me the address.

Patrice was curious to find out who this new woman was Roman wanted them to meet. She sat on her couch rubbing her belly as she dialed his number. When it went to voice mail she decided to let it go. Patrice's mind began to wander, *I hope he isn't thinking about replacing one of us. I'd kill that bitch before that happens.*

"Trish," Shayla whispered through the hallway.

Trish stepped out her office.

"Yes, dear?"

"Read these messages."

"You are lucky you're my girl because I would write your ass up. You haven't gotten any work done today," Trish said reading the messages. "Damn, girl what are you gone do?"

"I'm going to go over there."

"Do you want me to go with you?"

"No, maybe I should go alone. This is my headache."

"Are you sure? I'll go if you want me to."

"I'm positive."

"Okay, keep my number on speed dial in case I need to come beat a bitch ass!" Trish looked up to see Anthony standing at the door. "And if I have to come back in here again Shayla, I will write you up. No handling your personal affairs on the clock. Now log off of social media!" Trish said sternly hoping Anthony hadn't heard any of their conversation.

"Okay," Shayla said, "I don't feel good and I can't focus. Can I use a few personal hours, please?" Shayla said going along with Trish's story. She logged off the internet and opened up a file. "I'm almost done with the case notes now."

"Well it should have been done an hour ago!" Trisha yelled.

"Hey Trish, it's cool. I'll talk to her. Close that door behind you," Anthony said while walking toward Shayla.

"Did I do something wrong Anthony?"

"Yes, you did" Anthony responded sitting on her desk.

"I'm sorry."

"There's nothing to be sorry for unless there's nothing you can do about it."

Shayla had a look of confusion on her face.

"Don't look so confused" Anthony laughed. "Why don't you go shut the blinds cut the lights and lock the door."

Shayla smiled and said, "Oh I see." She shut the blinds and locked the door. "You sure you want the lights out?"

"Yes, I want them to think you're already gone for the day." Anthony stood up and slid his pants off while Shayla took off her dress. She bent over to take off her shoes. "Naw baby, leave those on."

Anthony sat back in the chair and she straddled herself

on top of him. She kissed his neck and shoulders and whispered in his ear how good it felt. He caressed her nipples with his tongue while rubbing her back and squeezing her ass and thighs.

"That's right baby," he moaned as Shayla gripped the back of the chair, moving up and down while squeezing her muscles wanting to feel every inch of him. When his legs began to shake she rode the tip of his dick and just as he came she slid back down on it. Anthony grabbed Shayla as she tried to get up.

"Come home with me?"

"I have plans tonight," Shayla was starting to like Anthony but those quick nuts he was shooting off wasn't enough to keep her interested in him long term. "Will you save me a piece of your peanut brittle for later?" she asked knowing he'd be confused.

"Peanut Brittle, I hope that's not what you're calling all this dick I've been giving you? I hate nuts!"

"I love nuts but I don't like them quick and easy to digest. I like my nuts to last for a while so I can savor them."

"Is that a complaint? If so, it can easily be fixed. Come home with me and I'll fix it now."

"I was hoping you said that but I really can't today."

"I'm not going to argue with you. At least promise me that this isn't the last time I'll get to spend time with you."

"I promise it's not." she lied. That quick nut he shot in her minutes ago was enough to make her remember that the only sugar covered quick nuts that she liked was bite-sized Sneakers, she was done looking for satisfaction in Mr. Brittle.

She pulled in her driveway and sat there for a while, wondering what life would be like if she was single. She wondered if what she planned to do was really worth all the trouble she was about to go through just for a little payback. As she thought of life without a husband Shayla heard arguing coming from inside the house. The longer she sat in the car the louder the voices seemed to get.

"Bitch you don't leave until I tell you to leave." Roman yelled.

Curious to see who Roman was talking to Shayla got out the car and crept to the door.

"I don't care how bad your feet hurt or how sore your pussy is. Make my fuckin' money before I come beat your ass."

At that moment everything started to click. *His ass is a pimp; damn Patrice must be his new bottom bitch if she's been around this long.* Shayla knew all she needed to know. She wasn't going to go to the club nor to Patrice's house to meet up with them. She didn't want to be seen associating with his hos, period. She unlocked the door and walked in.

"Let me call you back" Roman said while hanging up the phone.

"Who was that?" Shayla asked.

"Calvin."

"I've never heard that name, where'd you meet him at?"

"I met him around the corner at the store."

Shayla knew every word coming out of his mouth was a lie.

"Some friends invited me to come down to a club tonight. Do you want to go?"

"What club?" Roman asked taking a drink of water.

"Club swing or something like that."

Roman almost choked off the water he was drinking.

"Why do you want to go there and who invited you?"

"One of my clients invited me yesterday."

"What's her name?"

"Now you know I can't tell you that information. But she said it's off the chain so do you want to go or no?"

"Naw, I pass. But you aren't going either!"

"Yes I am".

Roman grabbed her by the arm.

"Look, I said you're not going down there!"

"Let go of my arm" Shayla yelled. Roman grabbed her arm tighter. "I said let me go!" She screamed with tears rolling down her eyes.

When he let go she grabbed her purse and ran out the door. She pulled up in front of Anthony's house unannounced. The porch light came on as she walked up the steps and Anthony opened the door.

"Why are you crying?"

"He, he…" Shayla stuttered.

"Did he hit you?" Anthony said enraged.

"No, he grabbed my arm."

Anthony looked at the now purple bruises on her arm. He took his phone out of his pocket and took pictures.

"You may need these in case you decide to go to the police."

"I don't need to; I just need a place to sleep for the night where I'll feel protected. I apologize for popping up."

"You were already invited to come. You can have my bed."

Shayla got into bed and passed out. When she woke up it was a little after midnight and Anthony was sleep on the couch. She walked over to him bent down and kissed him on the neck. She felt bad about the way she planned on doing him but what's the purpose of having a fuck buddy that always leaves you mad after you fuck? It wasn't that he didn't have enough, Anthony had dick for days. It wasn't that he didn't know how to use his tool, he was a handyman. Her only problem with him was his quick performance and only when he couldn't get it back up for an encore. He told her it was an easy fix and she wanted to see if that was true so she kissed his neck harder. He didn't move. She pulled his cover down. *Oh no underwear,* she thought and grabbed a handful of his dick. He didn't move.

Shayla kissed his chest, stomach and lips but he still didn't move. Feeling like she ran out of choices she put his dick down her throat and Anthony looked down at her with a smile.

"I should have known you were faking!" she said laughing once he was out of her mouth. "scoot over, I want to lay with you. Your bed is making me feel lonely.

Anthony made room for her to join him on the couch. He really wanted his dick sucked but she had him too excited too fast and he didn't want to nut fast. Shayla didn't realize it but she was the problem. Everything about her excited him in ways a woman had never done before and if she wasn't married he burn his player card for her. She was everything he wanted his woman to be and he'd take his time to show her that as she went through her divorce.

They shared a kiss that he hoped expressed to her that she was more than a new fuck friend before falling to sleep in each other's arms. Two hours later Anthony's phone started to ring off the hook. It was Trish.

"Have you seen Shayla?"

"Yeah she's right here."

"Let me talk to her please." he handed Shayla the phone.

"Hello?"

"Hey, wake up. Your husband is sitting outside of my house looking for you. I told him you left about ten minutes ago to go home."

"Okay, I'm on my way home right now."

Shayla flew out the door without given Anthony an explanation. Five minutes after getting home Roman came in.

"Where the fuck were you?"

Shayla didn't answer.

"Do you hear me talking to you?"

"I hear you." she said with caution.

"Well fuckin' answer me then!"

"Okay. I was with your baby mama Patrice, and your other three hos. Anything else you want to know?"

She couldn't hold it in and there was no way she'd let him scare her into staying with him. She was done with him.

"What the hell are you talking about Shayla?"

"I know all about your little club and the whores you're pimping from it. You have a daughter that's out there selling her pussy now because some sad way she learned about you pimping her mother."

There was nothing he could say in his defense so he shifted the subjected.

"So you went to the club?"

"Yeah, I went." she lied, "It's funny how they were trying to convince me to become one of your ho's until I let them know I was the bottom bitch for the past 16 years and that they work for me now!"

Shayla tired of all the bullshit and lies pulled the gun

she purchased almost a year ago out of her purse. It was supposed to be used for protection from her clients' abusers that she sent to jail but in the heat of the moment she found a new use for it. She pointed it at Roman, and fired one shot to the chest.

"You dirty, bitch" he said stumbling over.

"I guess I am because I never went to the club, or met with your hos. But you did put these bruises on me and pay back is a bitch".

Roman reached for his pocket and she took one last shot. Roman fell face first onto the waxed hardwood floor. Shayla then called the police and told them her husband had been beating her and that she'd shot him. She walked to her bedroom, stood in the doorway and slammed the door into her head. Then she slammed her hand in the door. She wanted to do more damage to herself but she had to know. The thought had been on her mind for almost three months. Before she ever knew that her husband had been cheating and before she ever slept with Anthony. She pulled out the pregnancy test she purchased two months ago and pee'd on the testing strip. In less than 30 seconds she was looking at two pink lines.

"Damn" she said holding back tears. After 16 years of being told she couldn't get pregnant, she was and without a doubt Roman was the father.

When she heard the sirens she threw the pregnancy test on top of Roman's bleeding body as he took he took his last few breaths. His final movement was him adjusting his head to see the test results.

Shayla whispered into her dead husband's ear with tears streaming down her face of both joy and pain, "Pay back is a greedy, bitch. She fucked us both!"

The End

My Football Candy Fantasy

"Girl, look at his yellow ass."

Kristiana nodded her head at one of the fathers sitting in the bleachers watching his son practice. She was supposed to be at her son, Jesse's, football practice to show support to the now 12th grade varsity player, but after seeing how packed the stands were with men, she brought her sister along for a game of, "I'd fuck him."

"Which one?" Lisa asked trying not to make it obvious that she too was on a mission to find her next good fuck in bleachers.

"Him bitch, the one who looks like he owns a barbershop or two. I can't really see his face from here but, there was something about him that has me wanting to see it. I don't know if it's the way he's swagging in his clothes, the confidence in his walk, or the fact that his body is sexy as hell."

It was like he had heard her as he stood up and began walking their way with a smile so bright it could melt honey, and their panties away.

"How are you doing ladies? Do y'all know if the concession stand is open? It's hot as hell out here today, I need a bottle of water. Would either of you like one, I got you if you do?" he offered looking from one woman to the next. "I love my nephew, but shit, I might go sit in my car with the A.C blasting."

"I love my nephew you too but I might have to join you in the car," Lisa said and an elbow from her sister forced her to clean up her words. "I mean, sit in my own car under the air conditioning and no, we will pass on the water. Think I'm thirsty for something else."

He looked into her eyes and wasn't sure what he was seeing back, but he knew it had a lot to do with getting in his car and nothing to do with water or air conditioning.

"Well, it was a pleasure meeting you both." he said in a slight humorous tone that projected his uncertainty.

"I'm Lisa and this is my sister Kristiana," Lisa extended her hand and then said, "And you are?"

"I'm Leonard and but you can call me Lee."

He accepted her hand in his and Lisa shook it longer than any handshake he ever was involved in. Lee had to give her hand a soft squeeze to get her to snap out of her trance. He wasn't more than twenty feet away before Lisa went in on him.

"I can tell you what it is about him, he's just sexy as hell," Lisa exclaimed followed by a laugh.

"I thought you didn't do light-brights? I thought that Milkduds over there would be more of your type." Kristiana replied pointing to the head coach Marcus.

Looking out at the field Lisa yelled, "Damn, look at his fine ass! He can be my coaching piece of milk chocolate. That's the type you give a small taste to now and then blow his mind later. that's how you keep him coming back."

"Speaking of now & laters, I never told you what happened the other night." Kristiana bragged.

"Ahh shit!" Lisa joked as she danced her way to take a seat. She could tell by her sister's last words it was going to be juicy.

"Girl, let me tell you. I came up to the school looking for Jesse the other night because he never came home nor did he call which wasn't like him. I drove around to all his usual spot and my last stop was the football field. Do you see that coach over there that's throwing passes to Jesse?"

"That tall chuck of brownie with the sun visor on? Yeah, I see him, why?"

"Well, that's coach Justin and he was on the football field using the boys practice dummies to work out, that night. I asked him if he'd seen him and he told that I had just missed him, and that Jesse was on his way home. As I started to walk away he called me back and asked me to wait because he needed to talk to me about something. Watching him work out on that field did something to me. I started getting hot between the legs and the longer I waited for him to finish the sexier he looked. About five minutes passed before he was done wiping the sweat off his chest with a towel. I didn't let him shit, I walked my fast ass right up to him and kissed him."

Kristiana paused in anticipation for Lisa's reaction but there wasn't one. Lisa's wow factor in her sister's actions when it came to men died years and she didn't put shit passed her after their vacation in Miami. After watching Kristiana blow two strangers they met on the beach as a third fucked her however he pleased from the back was enough proof that her sister wasn't afraid to let loose. Not saying that Lisa was a saint, she had blown and fucked all three men like her sister did too, and both woman credited there fuck fest to fun times in Miami.

Kristiana continued where she left off.

"Before I kissed I thought his dehydration from the workout would have his kiss tasting like that smell that grows behind your ear when you don't clean it but he still had the flavor from his red sports drink on his breath. Anyways, the next thing I knew he was bending me over the teams cooler and he entered me from behind. I yelled out in a pleasurable pain as he pulled my hair and slapped my ass. Girl, the negro had me calling his ass daddy! He sat on the cooler with dick standing tall as I got on top of it backward and saddled up. Bitch, I thought I was cow girl riding his chocolate stallion. Riding him for about four minutes, I started hearing the roar of thunder and a steady flow of rain dripped down my back. He didn't let the water stop us. He acted like we asked for it to rain as he kissed me on my neck telling me how good it felt as flashes of lightning struck. The drizzle of the rain quickly turned into drops belonging to a storm and then he asked me if I wanted him to stop."

"Yeah stop! Stop talking because I ain't been fucked in the rain yet and hearing this shit got me looking up at the clouds and ready to go find Lee." Lisa interrupted as she laughed.

"Nope I'm telling my story and you're going to listen. Where did I stop? Oh yeah, I was about to tell you that the shit felt so good and hurt so bad at the same time that all I could do was shake my head no. As soon as he put my nipple into his mouth the lights on the field pop on. Thinking we were caught, he tried to slid from under me so he pull his pants up and I was thinking hell naw, not today. I grabbed him by the hands and fell over to the field with his dick still inside of me. My face was in the turf with the weight of his body on my back. I didn't give a fuck about the mud I was laying in but he did. He flipped me over and when he stood up to look around to make sure we hadn't been caught I got on my knees and let him make love to my mouth. His thick rod hit the back of my throat and I gagged but he kept stroking. That freaky motherfucka called me every bitch in the book. You already know my nasty ass was loving every moment of that shit. I continued to suck on his dick until I caused his body to jerk and shake. He begged me to stop because he wanted to get back in this pussy before he nutted so I released him, licking my lips seductively. I was ready for the dick again but he said needed to tame this kitty with his tongue first. He got down and put his head between my thighs. As he sucked on my clit and played in my juices with one hand, he massaged my nipples with the other. My back arched as his tongue fluttered against my clit and his fingers probed in and out of my pussy until he found my spot. My body shook and I tried to snatched his fingers out determined to hold out just a little while longer, only for him to replace them with his tongue. My nails scratched the turf while I yelled out in pleasure. When his fingertip entered my ass I exploded like an erupting volcano. Not wanting to miss out on the fun I stood up and kissed him before he could swallow my juices,"

"Yous a freaky little bitch, Kris, but keep going. I'm about to erupt too." Lisa joked interrupting the erotic tale.

"Don't waste that nutt on your panties heffa, we're going to find you some dick out here. I'm almost finished with my story." she laughed and then concluded. "He was at full attention and ready to fuck! He tackled me into a missionary position with my legs spread and slid his thick horse inside me. Loving the aggression, I reach my hand under our connection and massaged his balls, making him moan out in pleasure. Thrusting harder and faster with sweat and rain dripping down his back, my juices added moisture as it leaked down my thighs. I whispered for him to turn me over but he didn't, instead he spread my legs as wide as they will go, turned me over and licked on my pussy again. I moved his head and motioned for him to come closer. Looking him in his eyes, I lift my legs onto his shoulders. I tightened my muscles against his dick and I knew he was about to cum. I squeezed harder, looked at him and screamed you're my candy fantasy coach, as we came together."

Krisitiana looked at her sister and in unison they both screamed out in laughed. It took two minutes before Lisa could get herself together to talk.

"What in the fuck is a candy fantasy?"

"I don't know what the hell it is but when you got a sexy ass coach fucking the shit out of you in the rain on a football, screaming the shit, just felt right."

The End

Tootsie Pop

I sat in my seat staring at this fine chunk of chocolate on stage. I watched his Tootsie Pop swing in circles inside the white G-string he wore as he walked toward me. The spinning tassels were beginning to hypnotize me as I stood from my seat. I rocked my hips to the beat of the music. My mouth watered as freaky thoughts consumed my mind. My knees got weak from the smell of his cologne. He soaked my neck with his beads of sweat as he whispered in my ear, "Do you like what you see baby?"

I shook my head yes as he ran his hand between my legs. He pretended to suck my imaginary juices from his fingers. The crowd of women began to scream his name as he grabbed me forcefully and flipped me over into a doggy-style position. Not wanting to lose my balance I quickly grabbed the railing in front of me. The women got louder with every thrust against my ass. This shit was turning me on and I wanted him in the worst way.

I started having flashbacks of his tootsie pop being in my mouth the night before. The way he looked at me fill of lust as I licked his shaft up and down before spitting on it and putting it into my mouth encouraged me to keep going. Him pulling my hair during his final thrust reminded me of the way he pulled my hair while yelling out that I was the best he ever had. See, we had this bet that it would take me less than five licks to get to the center of his tootsie pop coating my throat. He claimed no one could take him there because he had dick control. And well, me being the bitch I am, and knowing what this mouth can do, I was up for the challenge. I lost my train of thought as his last thrust sent me stumbling into the line of ladies waiting to get their turn.

All I heard was, "That's right girl," and "You took that dick bitch!" from my friends. I took my seat and continued to think about the night before. Me stumbling reminded me of how quickly his knees buckled when I laid him down and did pushups on him with my face while still sucking his dick.

"Got damn girl you can suck a dick," is what he said as I devoured him whole, allowing my tongue to make swirls on his sack. Shortly after he squealed, "damn bitch" as I sucked the soul from his dick as he came down my throat.

I was snapped out of my thoughts as the MC said, "How many licks does it take to get to the center of the Tootsie Pop?". I smiled knowing between him and I, it only took three.

The End

THE PENSTRESS

Prison Break

It had been three months since Angie saw Fahiem. The last argument with him put her in a place she wish it hadn't. She thought back to the beginning. Leaving town was her first mistake. After stepping out the box and trying something different, letting her heart lead her was the second. The third mistake was showing him how much she cared and her jealous side. Angie believed in letting those she loved and cared for know just how much, but Fahiem was different. He wasn't the type of guy she was used to. He was strong willed and very blunt. A like it or leave it type of guy. Angie was used to calling all the shots in her relationships and Fahiem was a challenge. But deep down he was just what she wanted. She wanted a man to make decisions and shut her down when she was out of control. Not one to put hands on her or tell her what to do but one she couldn't run over. She was tired of the men that did what she said when she said. Fahiem just coming out of a relationship wanted just the opposite. He was just looking for someone to have fun with. He didn't want anything serious.

Fahiem was tall and muscular with dimples to die for. His smile melted your heart. And it didn't hurt that he was a flirt. Angie was shy and laid back. Usually didn't speak until spoken to. Short thin and as sweet as pie. Angie loved helping others. She was very passive and forgiving.

Angie thought back to the argument that made her say she was done with him. If she could go back she would have said nothing. Angie wanted more than just a casual sex relationship with Fahiem. She let her jealousy get the best of her.

Angie sat at the bar sipping her Hennessey and coke with her eyes glued on the woman all in Fahiem's face. She was a beautiful chocolate sister with hazel eyes but in

Angie's eyes no one in the club even came close to her. She was 5'1 in height, shaped like a coke bottle and gorgeous golden brown eyes.

Unable to contain herself she sat her now empty glass back on the bar and walked toward Fahiem who was headed her way.

"So, who was that bitch?"

"What bitch Ang?"

"The hazel eyed bitch that was all up in yo fucking face," she yelled.

"Man, I talked to that girl for two minutes," he responded shaking his head.

"Two minutes too long," Angie responded sarcastically.

Fahiem laughed. "You aren't my girl so honestly I can be all up on whomever I want."

"I know I'm not your girl but she's taking my place. The time you used to spend with me you now spend with her."

"I spend time with you. Maybe if you stopped tripping and acting jealous all the damn time I would spend more time with you."

"I don't need this shit," Angie said snatching her purse from the bar and walking toward the door.

She walked to her car as fast as she could with Fahiem following close behind.

"You just remember this," she said now facing him.

"I have always been there when you needed me. When I didn't have it, I would make a way to get it but I guess that's not enough for you. What have you ever done for me? Tell me one fucking thing that you've done for me?"

Fahiem just stood there looking at her.

"Well?" Angie said.

"You can't because you haven't."

Tears ran down her face. Fahiem took her face into his hands and kissed her on her forehead. "Angie you know I care about you."

Angie snatched away from him.

"Fuck You!" she said as she got in her car and pulled off.

Angie didn't know where to go. She had no one. She drove from Los Angeles to Las Vegas. She called up her girl Stacy she went to high school with. Angie spent six months in Vegas at Stacy's. She often thought about calling Fahiem and apologizing for the things she said but she also felt like he was using her at times. After six months of dancing and saving money Angie left Vegas and headed back to Los Angeles. She called up Andrew and he said she could stay with him for a while. She made Andrew promise not to tell Fahiem she was coming back.

Angie hadn't been back a week when a man in his twenties robbed and attempted to rape her. She was walking to her car after dancing at Andrew's and the man came out of nowhere and robbed her by gunpoint. After taking her money he pinned Angie against the car with one hand while using the other to snatch her pants down. Fahiem heard screaming and when he was close enough to see that it was Angie he lost it and beat the man unconscious.

After that incident Angie and Fahiem were inseparable. They moved in together and Angie went back to school. She didn't have to worry about anything. Fahiem was a good provider and protector. Their friendship outweighed their relationship. Nine months after moving in with Fahiem, Angie received a phone call from jail. It was

Fahiem.

"Hey baby it's me."

"What the hell, why are you in jail?"

"They pulled me over for a busted tail light and when they ran my information they said I had a no bail warrant. After they booked me I found out that the guy that robbed you died from the beating I gave him."

"Oh my God...baby I'm sorry. This is all my fault."

"No, it's not I had a choice and the choice I made was to beat his ass. As soon as I find out when I'm going to court I will let you know."

"What can I do to help you?" Angie cried.

"There's nothing you can do. Baby don't cry. I love you."

"I love you too."

That was the first time Fahiem said those words to Angie. She knew she loved him but because of how their relationship started she didn't want him to think she was saying it because he was her hero.

Three months later Fahiem was sentenced to two years in prison for manslaughter. When Angie heard the news, she felt like she'd been stabbed in the heart. Fahiem had money stashed but it wasn't enough to get her through two years. She decided to use the money that was stashed to support Fahiem while he locked down and she would start dancing again to support herself. Andrew promised Fahiem he would look after Angie, so he had her move in with him until Fahiem came home. Another three months went by before Angie went to see Fahiem. She sent letters twice a week faithfully and kept money on his books. Angie got on the bus and as they pulled up to his block her stomach turned. She stepped into the room full of women and children waiting to see their loved ones. There were cribs lined against two of the walls and school desks filled the room. There were vending machines to purchase food and drinks and microwaves as well. There were deputies at each door. Angie looked around the room for Fahiem. She didn't see him. She sat in the seat closet to the door. Three minutes later the door opened and there he was smiling. He stopped at a desk and spoke briefly to a deputy. The tears ran down her face as she watched him walk toward her, his head held high. He wore blue pants with a huge C.D.C going down the left pant leg, a matching blue shirt with a white tee underneath and beige boots that resembled timberlands. His hair and beard were freshly cut. Even in his prison attire his swag was on point.

He stopped at their table and pulled her up from her seat and into his arms. Her knees weakened as he tilted his head downward and kissed her with so much passion that she started to cream her panties. Pulling away from her, Fahiem took his seat.

"I'm glad you made it. I was scared you would chicken out," he said laughing.

"I'd go to the end of earth for you baby," she said crying.

He wiped the tears from her eyes.

"Don't cry I'm fine. If we could go back I wouldn't change a thing. Well yeah, I would. I would have been licensed so the beating could have been legal." Angie laughed.

Angie noticed tables and benches outside on a huge patio surrounded by at tall gate.

"Are we allowed to go out there," she asked curiously.

"Yeah come on let's go," he said grabbing her hand and leading the way. There was a bench off in the cut. As they got up one of the deputies nodded his head to Fahiem. "Why is he doing that are we in trouble?" Angie asked scared.

"No," he said pinching her nipple.

Angie stared at him and tried to think of things to say to detour her from getting horny.

"We good, that's my home boy's brother. I told him you were coming and if I slipped him a fifty he'd let me get a quickie."

Angie blushed.

"Well, we don't want to waste anytime do we?"

Fahiem smiled. That smile melted her heart. Angie sat on Fahiem's lap. He slipped his hand up her skirt and pulled her G-string to the side. She rose up as if she were fixing her dress and slid on top of his dick. It had been six months since they had sex and it was tight. She slowly moved side to side to try and loosen up. After getting it all the way in she worked her hips around while squeezing her muscles. She could feel his pulse as he came. She squeezed as hard as she could while getting up not wanting to leave a drip of evidence on him. Angie went to the restroom and slipped the deputy a fifty.

As she waited for a deputy to let her back into the visiting room she noticed Fahiem had left the patio area and was now seated at their table.

"I don't want you to come back tomorrow," Fahiem said caressing the top of her hand.

"I want you to go home in the morning. Make a copy of the house key and give it to Ricky."

"Your brother Ricky?"

"Yes. He's going to stay at the house until I get home. Don't worry about the rent or bills he will take care of that."

They talked a little more, ate, and said their goodbyes. While on the bus a deputy sat next to Angie.

"Did you go to Crenshaw?" the deputy asked.

"Yes I did."

"What's up Tasha?"

"Girl I thought that was you. I wasn't even paying attention I'm sorry."

"Who are you visiting?" Tasha asked.

"My boyfriend Fahiem."

"Why is he here?"

Angie told Tasha the story of what happened, and Tasha told her she could hook her up with a job in the prison if she applied and went to training.

"I'll think about it."

"Either way give me a call girl."

"I will. It was nice seeing you."

Angie called Tasha the very next day. While catching up on the past she made sure to tell Tasha she signed up for the class and would start training within the next two weeks.

"Okay when you're training is done let me know and I will take care of the rest," Tasha said before hanging up.

Angie wrote Fahiem a letter telling him the things she wanted to tell him when she was in Vegas.

"Dear Fahiem, I know in the past I've let my jealous ways detoured you from wanting to pursue a relationship with me. I can't see myself with anyone but you. I lay up at night wondering what my life would be like with you in it. I wish I could turn the hands of time so that I would have met you years ago, But I can't. All I can do at this point is show you how much I love you and far I'd go to make you happy if you give me the chance. I love you and I'll see you soon."

Angie didn't tell Andrew what she was doing until her training was over and she was hired.

"You don't have a mean bone in your body, be careful," Tasha told Angie.

"They will try to manipulate you and set you up. Stay on your P's and Q's and remember never to tell anyone any of your personal business. These men will try to befriend you. Don't fall for it. Watch your back at all times. They don't give a fuck about you."

Just as Tasha promised Angie landed work at the same prison Fahiem was in. They teamed up the newbies with experienced correctional officers. And again as Tasha promised they were teamed together. Angie often wondered what it was Tasha was doing to get so much love. She hoped to get even a glimpse of Fahiem. For two weeks she didn't see him at all. Then one day Tasha told her they were moving to another quad. It was lights out and Tasha and

Angie went cell to cell making sure everyone was in order. Just as she got to the end of the hall she heard Angie. She turned around to see no one. She heard it again. She turned back around and there was Fahiem. She walked over to his cell. Instantly her heart dropped. The look on his face said it all.

"What the fuck are you doing here?" he whispered.

Angie explained how she went through training and got hired.

"Why would you put your life in danger like this? All I asked you to do was write me."

"There you go trying to run shit." Fahiem shouted.

"Baby I'm sorry and I wasn't and I'm not trying to run shit. I just wanted to be here for you," Angie explained.

"Good night," was all he said before Angie could get another word out.

"Tasha, why didn't you tell me this was his quad?"

"I wanted to surprise you."

"Girl, I appreciate it but he's pissed."

"Why didn't he know what you were doing?"

"No I didn't tell him because I knew he would say no."

"Oh shit, I'm sorry I was only trying to help. I've been in the same situation and someone helped me out".

Angie looked at her.

"Don't tell anyone but my dad is the warden."

Now it all made sense. All the special treatment and favors she was given.

"I could be killed if the inmates were to find out so promise me you won't utter a word to anyone!"

"I promise, I won't."

"Good, now get back in there and see your man. I got your back. So hurry and don't take all day." Angie walked back to the cell.

"Man go on I'm sleep."

"Baby I'm sorry."

Angie opened the cell and went in. She looked at his cell mate and yelled,

"Get up and lay on the floor face down!"

Then she looked at Fahiem.

"Get up."

When he did she put his pants down while dropping to her knees. She ran her tongue up and down the shaft then sucked gently on the head. She put her hands around it and sucked up and down taking him in deeper each time. Placing both hands on his behind and squeezing gently and she took as much of him in as she could she topped him off hands-free as he exploded in her mouth. She looked up at him after swallowing and he ~~put~~ pulled her up. After unbuttoning her shirt he wrapped his arm around her waist and seductively slid his finger between her ~~her~~ lips and thrusted ever so gently. Grabbing a fist full of hair and pulling making her back arch while delivering a quivering injection of his ego inside of her, like an inner massage.

Angie quickly pulled her pants up and adjusted her shirt. She noticed his cell mate watching as she kissed Fahiem goodbye. On her way out she slapped his cell mate Chris on the ass, bent down and whispered in his ear, "the next time you peak I'll tell Fahiem."

Angie continued to sneak into Fahiem's cell night after night. One night during sex Angie threw up. Fahhiem stopped and asked, "Are you okay?"

'I think I'm getting the flu. I've been sick lately."

"Well stay away from me I don't want to get sick," he

said rubbing his hand along her cheek.

"Babe I have to go," Angie whispered.

He kissed her on the forehead and she left. Before she could get out the module she threw up two more times.

"You need to go to the doctor," Tasha told her.

"I will as soon as I get off. Angie clocked out and went straight to the store for a pregnancy test." When she got home she took the test and paced back and forth waiting five minutes for the results to pop up. Two pink lines. "Damn" Angie said crying. She knew she couldn't work while pregnant. She called the prison and talked to her supervisor. Damn, how am I going to tell this to Fahiem, it would kill him knowing that he wouldn't be home for the baby's birth. She decided to write a letter because telling him in person would be impossible.

"Tasha, will you do me a favor and get this letter to

Fahiem?"

"Why don't you take it with you to work?" Tasha asked.

"I'm not going to work because I'm pregnant."

"Awe, I'm so happy for you. Okay I will pick it up in the morning."

Tasha picked up the letter and gave it to Fahiem the next morning.

"Thank you" he said, while turning his head in disgust.

"No problem sexy."

Fahiem pretended not to hear her.

"I never realized how sexy you were until now. Now I know why Angie went through all the trouble she did."

"Thank you," he said turning around.

Fahiem sat on his bunk and opened the letter.

"Dear Fahiem, I don't know any other way to tell you but like this. I'm pregnant. I can't work pregnant so I'll be home until the baby is born. So until I start to show I will be working at Andrew's. I am three months and will have my first ultrasound next week. I will be sure to send pictures; I figured you would wonder why I hadn't been there. I can't visit, so I will write. I love you, Angie."

A few nights passed before Tasha went to Fahiems cell. Fahiem sat up.

"Hey Fa."

"What's up Tasha?" he replied.

"That's what I came to see."

"What are you talking about?"

"This is how it's going to work. You are going to fuck me twice a week until you get out of here. And if you don't I will go to the warden and let him know that Angie was creeping in here at night. And now she's pregnant with your baby. I'll have both your asses behind bars."

"Bitch you crazy," Fahiem said, "get the fuck outta here."

"If you think I'm playing then try me." Tasha said.

Fahiem wanted to beat Tasha's ass but instead he put his head down.

"Alright," Fahiem said.

But let's be clear this is for her not you."

"Whatever," she said. "Now pull it out so I can see what you workin' with." Fahiem pulled his soft dick out but that only made Tasha smile. She got on her knees and the more she licked and sucked the harder it was for Fahiem to resist. He closed his eyes and pretended she was Angie. His dick got harder and harder. He pulled her hair as he came and she almost choked. Next time pull harder she said sarcastically. She got up and winked on her way out.

Fahiem was all fucked up in the head. He didn't know what to do. He loved Angie and he couldn't tell her with her being pregnant. Three days later Tasha handed Fahiem a letter from Angie.

"You owe me for this," Tasha said handing him the letter.

He opened it. It was a plain piece of paper that said, "I love you."

There were three pictures of the ultrasound.

"P.S. the next one will be in four weeks. I will send you more and keep you updated."

There was a kiss in lipstick and the scent of Angie's perfume. After putting her pictures on the wall he laid back on his black and deep thought about his life and what he wanted to do when he touched down.

Later that night he was awakened by the sound of Tasha enter the cell before he could sit up to see what was going on.

"Sit on the toilet," she demanded.

When he didn't budge she ~~put~~ pulled out her baton, hit it against the palm of her hand and said it again.

"I said sit on the toilet, I feel like riding!"

Fahiem did as she said. This time he planned not to think of Angie at all. But to think of and treat her as the whore she was. She sat on his lap and rode him for what seemed like hours. Then she turned around and rode just the tip of his dick. He grabbed her by the throat as he came. She got up. "Don't ever do that shit again," Tasha said after slapping him.

"That's how I get down, Angie likes it. Isn't that who you want to be?"

She looked at him like she wanted to kill him. She put her pants on and walked out.

Fahiem was stressed out dealing with Tasha. Every time she saw him outside the cell she would wink. He struggled with the thought of telling Angie what was going on but didn't want to upset or stress her out. Four weeks later just as promised Angie sent Fahiem more pictures of the baby. There was also a letter attached.

"Hey baby. I love you. Your little girl is doing well. She's growing and kicking like crazy. I got your letter. Good idea sending it to Andrew. How is it that you will be home so soon? Not that I care because I am ecstatic you'll be here for the baby's birth. I hope Tasha is taking good care of you in there. I love you and I will always be here for you. I'm here to support, compromise, and learn from the mistakes we've made. I know it's my fault you're in there and I promise to make it up to you. You are my heart.

Love, Angie."

Weeks went by and to his surprise he didn't see Tasha. Some people said she got fired. Others say she transferred. Either way he was happy her ass was gone. He spent the next four months mapping out a plan for his future. He was determined to give Angie the man she deserved. Fahiem was released early and couldn't wait to get home to see Angie. He didn't tell her the exact date he was getting out because he wanted to surprise her. He had Ricky pick him up. Angie wasn't home when he got there so he took a bath put on fresh clothes shaved and laid on the couch. When she walked in she dropped her bags and ran. Fahiem hugged her tight and kissed her. Then he stood back and looked at her belly. He lifted her shirt and kissed her stomach.

"Hi baby girl, this is daddy. I can't wait to meet you."

"I took pictures every two weeks so you could see how

I changed. Andrew is on his way over."

"I wondered why he didn't answer his phone."

"He has a surprise for you."

"What is it?"

"Wait and see."

Two hours passed before Andrew pulled up. He walked into the house and Fahiem almost choked on his drink when he saw Tasha with him.

"Hey Fa," Tasha said.

"Long time no see."

"Hi Tasha." Fahiem replied.

Andrew hugged him and pointed to Tasha's stomach.

"It looks like we have something in common."

Fahiem looked at him like he was crazy.

"Baby," Andrew said to Tasha, "turn sideways. She's five months with a baby boy."

"Wow," Fahiem said.

"I'll be right back."

Fahiem went into his bedroom, closed the door and paced back and forth wondering what he should do. Five months ago he was having sex with her twice a week no condom. His stomach turned into knots.

Angie peeked her head through the door.

"Baby are you okay? You've been in here for a while now."

"Yeah I'm good," he said walking out the room. "I'm glad you guys came by, congrats on the baby but I need to get some sleep I'm not feeling too good."

"Okay call me later or stop by the club."

"Alright," Fahiem replied.

With Fahiem facing Andrew and Tasha behind Andrew's back; Tasha looked at Fahiem and mouthed "It's your baby."

Fahiem walked back in the house and slammed the door.

"Why did you do that?" Angie asked.

"What's wrong with you?"

"I hate that bitch," Fahiem said with hatred in his voice.

"How did he meet her anyway?"

"I introduced them."

"What the fuck for?"

"Hold up I ain't did shit to you so you need to watch your tone of voice and how you're talking to me. Now you can tell me what the hell is wrong with you or shut the hell up."

Fahiem walked into the room and shut the door. He sat on the bed with his head in his hands. Angie walked in. She stood in front of him and held him.

"I'm sorry I yelled at you. I don't know what's wrong with you. I'll leave for a while and give you some time to yourself."

Angie turned to walk away when Fahiem grabbed her arm.

"No, baby don't go sit down."

"Why are you treating Tasha like that after all the things she did for you while you were in jail?"

"Things like what rape me?"

"What do you mean rape me?"

"That's what I call it when you have sex against your will."

"Wait a minute. She forced you to have sex with her?"

"She said if I didn't fuck her twice a week she would go to the warden and tell him you were sneaking into my cell having sex with me and that you were pregnant. And for every letter you wrote I had to pay for it."

"By having sex with her?"

Angie grabbed her stomach.

"Why didn't you tell me babe?"

"I didn't want this to happen."

Fahiem said helping her to sit down.

"I'm fine. She just kicked me kind of hard. So you mean to tell me that the baby she's pregnant with could be yours?"

"Yes."

"What the fuck. You lying ass sack of shit. Get your shit and get the fuck out my house. You must have liked it in order for you not to say shit. You could have told me this shit a long time ago."

"What was telling you or anyone else for that matter going to do? The warden is her fuckin' daddy," Fahiem yelled.

"You know what just get out. I don't want to talk to or see you right now!"

She threw her car keys at him, watched him sped off then called Tasha.

"Hey Angie, what's up?" Tasha answered.

"I need you guys to turn around and come back. We need to talk."

"About what is something wrong?"

"No everything's fine."

"As a matter of fact come alone. I don't want to talk in front of Andrew. You know he will go back and tell Fahiem everything we say."

"Okay cool. I'll see you soon."

"Bitch," Angie said as she hung up the phone.

She went to the closet and pulled out her little black box. She sat on the couch in front of the door and sat it on her lap.

"I got you bitch," she said out loud while tapping on it.

The End

ABOUT THE AUTHOR

Keisha Davis was born and raised in South Central Los Angeles. She now resides in Palmdale , California with her children. She enjoys reading writing and spending time with her grandchildren. Reading on a sixth grade level in third grade Keisha began writing short stories, letters and poems for her friends and family. Keisha started writing her first book while at work and with the encouragement of co-workers and family began her search for a publisher. It would be three years before finding and being welcomed into the Conglomerate Ink family where she is currently working on her next book.